DO HARM

ER CRIMES
BOOK 4

RADA JONES MD

APOLODOR

APOLODOR PUBLISHING

DO HARM

PROLOGUE

The ship's rocking lulled Nadja to sleep. She closed her eyes, wrapped her left arm around his waist and snuggled until their bodies touched from head to toe to steal his warmth. His skin smelled like bittersweet aftershave and lovemaking. She smiled and planted a kiss on his shoulder.

"I love you. Isn't it wonderful to be together like this?"

"Yes."

Nadja sighed. "I'm so tired of hiding! I can't wait to be together all the time, day and night. Just think about all the places we'll go and all the things we'll do. I'll make you breakfast, and we'll walk hand in hand on the beach, and we'll play ball with the kids... How many children do you want?"

His body tightened. "Children?"

"Yes. I'd like two. A boy and a girl would be ideal, but I wouldn't mind having just boys. They have it easier. That's why I don't want two girls. A woman's life is always harder."

"I bet."

He threw off the sheets and sat up, escaping the arm

trying to hold him back, then pulled up his scrub pants and T-shirt and turned to the door.

"Where are you going?"

"Back to my cabin. I remembered something I need to do. I'll see you tomorrow."

"But... whatever it is that you must do, can't it wait until tomorrow? We were having so much fun!"

He shook his head. "I'm sorry, it can't. See you tomorrow, beautiful!"

"Gimme a kiss, at least," she said, uncovering her breasts and puckering her lips to entice him.

He sighed and leaned over for a quick kiss. Nadja wrapped her arms around his neck and wouldn't let go.

He laughed and pulled back. "See you tomorrow."

When the heavy metal door slammed behind him, Nadja rearranged her pillow and smiled, basking in the afterglow of their lovemaking. Even her windowless cabin felt cozy instead of cramped now that it smelled like him. She couldn't wait until they could sleep together through the night, wake up in each other's arms, and...

Someone knocked at the door.

Nadja glanced at her phone. Almost midnight. Who on earth could be coming so late? An emergency? But she wasn't on call. And even if she were, they wouldn't come to her cabin. They'd page her.

Another knock, louder now.

It's got to be him. He finished whatever he had to do, and he's back.

She jumped out of bed and opened the door, wearing nothing but a smile.

"Hi, Nadja. You have a moment?"

It wasn't him.

"Now? It's so late!"

"Look what I got you!"

Nadja glanced at the unopened bottle of Stolichnaya and sighed. She didn't want vodka. If she couldn't be with him, she'd rather be alone to remember his touch and dream about the days when they wouldn't hide anymore.

But she couldn't say no to her little elf. God only knows how her *Karlik* managed to get hold of that bottle of Stolichnaya. Certainly not in the crew mess, where the only thing stronger than beer was some Vietnamese liquor smelling like bug juice and strong enough to strip paint.

Nadja pulled on the crumpled T-shirt she'd thrown on the floor and opened the door to let *Karlik* in.

"How on earth did you get it?"

Karlik laughed. "It wasn't easy. I almost had to sell my soul to get it, but I did it for you. I know you miss home, and I wanted to get you something special. How are you doing?"

She got two coffee mugs from the bathroom, filled them, and handed one to Nadja. They sat next to each other on the crumpled sheets that still smelled like him. *Karlik* smiled.

The crystal-clear vodka burned Nadja's throat and warmed her inside. She shuddered. "*Na Zdorovié!* This is real!"

"Of course, it's real. Only the best for you, my friend. Especially now. You know, Nadja, I've been worried about you."

"About me? Why?"

"You just... don't seem to be yourself lately. You seem preoccupied. The other day, you forgot about that insulin. Yesterday you were late for the morning clinic. Half of the time, you don't even hear me speak to you. That's so not like you."

She refilled the cups.

"Is something bothering you? Trouble at home? You know you can tell me."

Nadja laughed.

"No trouble. I'm good. Very good, in fact."

"Tell me."

Nadja hesitated. But then, why not? For weeks, she'd been bursting to tell the whole world, let alone her best friend. And the vodka made it easier. She was tired of hiding. And why should she?

"OK, I'll tell you. But you have to promise not to tell anyone. It's a secret."

Karlik's fingers drew a cross over her lips, swearing to keep the secret.

Nadja sighed. "I'm getting married."

Karlik's jaw fell. "You are? Really? Congratulations! I'm so glad for you! Who's the lucky man?"

"That, I can't tell you. Not yet."

"When?"

"We... we haven't yet set a date."

"Why not?"

"He's... he needs to finalize his divorce first."

Karlik nodded. "I see. Well then, let's drink to that."

Nadja drained her cup. *Karlik* refilled it.

"That's why it's a secret? Because he's married?"

"That too. But even more because of the job. You know the company policy forbids relationships between coworkers. Sure, they don't care if you're discreet and don't create a scandal, but he's married, and flaunting it would get us in trouble. They'd send one of us on another ship or even fire us. Either way, we'd be separated, and that's the last thing we want."

"Of course. I understand. Here's to love and eternal happiness," *Karlik* said, refilling the mugs.

I shouldn't drink anymore, Nadja thought. But *Karlik* touched her mug to hers again, and it's bad luck not to drink after a toast. So she took another sip.

She wavered and grabbed onto the bed. She shook her head to clear it, but that didn't help. Her vision was blurry, like she was underwater.

"Are you OK?" *Karlik* asked.

Nadja nodded.

"Just... tired. I'm just tired," she mumbled.

"Let's put you to bed, then. But finish your drink first."

Nadja wanted to say no, but she didn't get to. *Karlik* brought the mug to her lips and made her drain it, then helped her lie down in bed.

Nadja laughed. "The bed feels like it's moving."

"Sure, it's moving. We're on a boat, remember?"

"On a boat?"

"Yes. We're on the *Sea Horse*. You forgot?"

"I..."

She closed her eyes, but the cabin started spinning, and a wave of nausea hit her hard. She opened her eyes and anchored them on the dark TV on the desk. Her nausea abated, but not much.

"I don't feel so good. I think I need to puke."

Karlik touched her shoulder.

"I'm so sorry. You drank too fast. Let me give you something to make you better."

"I... Thank you."

Nadja took a deep breath, and her eyes closed against her will.

I need to open them, or I'll puke.

"There, now."

Something sharp pricked the inside of her elbow. She tried to pull her arm, but *Karlik* held it tight.

"Relax, my friend. You'll feel much better in a moment. Count to ten."

"One. Two. Three. Four..."

Through the deep fog inside her head, she heard a door slamming and wondered who that was.

Then her body grew lighter and lighter. She floated like a feather, up to the sky, into a sea of brightness. And she thought no more.

CHAPTER 1

The sun isn't yet all the way up over the Sydney Harbor, but the day promises to be scorching. The soft asphalt gives under Emma's feet, and the city streets already smell like hot concrete.

Slender gray egrets with curious eyes rummage for food in last night's street party remains. The slender palms throw skinny shadows that tremble in the wind. Harried professionals stride toward their jobs without glancing at each other like morning commuters do in every metropolis in the world. But here, down under, they're tall, quiet, and mostly Asian.

I wonder why, Emma thinks, fighting with her soft roll-on. The stubborn wheels won't jump the curb to let her join the dozen other travelers waiting for the bus in the cheap hotel's parking lot. Emma swears between her teeth and pulls harder. The roll-on gives in, and she heads toward the others, wondering who they are.

She knows they're going to the *Sea Horse*, Aurora Cruise Company's newest cruise ship. Just like her, they're waiting for the bus to take them to the port for their new contract. But who are they?

The bus is late, so Emma distracts herself by trying to guess what they do. The five young Indonesians laughing and chatting must be cabin stewards. Or waiters. The three blonde Russians carrying their instruments have to be musicians. She can't place the sharp-dressed graying black man with a silver roll-on. He looks too old to be crew. A performer, maybe? Magician or pianist? He wouldn't cart a piano, but that bag is big enough for a tall hat, a pack of cards, and even a fluffy white rabbit.

A beautiful black girl with a huge blonde Afro struggles to drag her roll-on over the curb. The wheels resist, so she pulls harder. The handle breaks, and the roll-on crashes to the ground. The bag splits open, spilling its insides on the asphalt.

The parking lot fills with the heavy scent of perfume, so strong it makes Emma cough. The stricken girl stares at a broken bottle of Fendi, and her face drops. She looks like she's about to cry, but she bites her lip and kneels by the curb to gather a rainbow of perfume-soaked clothes covered in glass shards.

"Let me help," Emma says. She tries to stick with the less personal things, like a pair of red high heels and some ripped jeans, but she still gets to pick a pair of black lacy thongs and a toothbrush. She drops them in the bag as fast as she can, but the lock is broken, and the bag won't close anymore.

The girl starts sobbing just as the bus arrives.

The driver opens the luggage compartment, and the people line up to drop their bags and climb in. The bus fills up as Emma and the girl stare at the open roll-on.

It looks like an eviscerated trauma victim, with all the

innards tangled inside, Emma thinks. She'd love to leave the girl and get on the bus. But she can't.

"I have an idea. May I?"

She rummages through the clothes for a pair of leggings. She closes the bag and ties the leggings around it with a double knot after passing them through the handle so they can't slip off.

"It's not pretty, but it should hold until the ship. Let's carry it together. You don't want to have those leggings take all the weight."

They carry it in, then board the bus. They're the last ones, of course, and all eyes follow them to the empty seats in the back.

"Thank you."

"No problem."

Emma drops into the first empty seat. The girl sits next to her.

"Thank you so much. I don't know what I would have done without you."

"You'd have managed just fine."

"No, I wouldn't. I'd have collapsed there crying if it wasn't for you."

Emma sighs, wishing that, just this once, she'd minded her own business. There were plenty of people there who could have helped, but she had to do it, and now she's stuck with this girl who won't stop talking. After handling the perfume-soaked clothes, her hands smell like a whore-house, and she can already tell she's getting a migraine. And that's the last thing she needs today when she ought to focus and control her panic. But it's too late. Her head's pounding, her heart's racing, and her mouth is so dry she can't swallow.

"This is my first contract on a ship, and I'm terrified," the girl says.

Welcome to my world, Emma thinks. She asks, "What will you do on the ship?"

"My name is Gloria. I'm a singer."

"How lovely. I'm Dr. Steele. I'll be the ship doctor."

"You're a real doctor? With needles and stuff? Not the priest or the naturalist or something?"

"No priest. Needles and stuff."

"Wow. How long have you been a ship doctor?"

"I'm starting today. How about you? How long have you been a singer?"

"Oh, I've sung since I was a kid. But finding a gig is hard these days unless you get to know the right people. Back home, I could barely make enough to live on. But I really wanted to see the world, so I auditioned for ACC, and they offered me a contract. You make like no money, but you get free room and board, and you get to see amazing places. I've never been to Australia before. Have you?"

"No. Where are you from, Gloria?"

"Zimbabwe. You?"

"America."

"New York?"

"Sort of. New York state, not the city. It's up north, near Canada."

"Wow! I always wanted to go there someday. New York, that is."

"I bet someday you will."

When the bus finally stops at the cruise terminal, a couple of helpful young men offer to help Gloria with her luggage, and Emma sighs with relief. She gets her bag and drags it to an empty corner of the vast hangar that serves as a waiting room. She sits by the window, closes her eyes, and starts practicing circular breathing to slow down her heart.

Minutes later, she's settled enough to open her eyes and

watch the crowd, and it's worth it. Dozens of joyous reunions all over the room — laughing young men that hug and slap each other's back, happy to be together again.

The distinguished black man sits in the chair next to Emma's.

"Aren't they lovely? They're like kids coming home for Christmas. They're happy to be here. The *Sea Horse* is a good ship."

"You know them?"

"I met some of them on my previous trips." He extends a warm, firm hand. "I'm Will."

"I'm Emma."

"The doctor?"

"How did you know?"

His eyes sparkle with amusement.

"My powerful deductive skills. You aren't crew. You're too old to be an entertainer. You don't look like a personal trainer, and you don't carry a musical instrument. You don't wear a uniform, so you're not one of the officers. That narrows it down."

"That's pretty good."

"Isn't it? But to be honest, I happen to have inside knowledge. There she is."

A pale redhead with wild curls and not a shadow of a smile stops before Emma. Her white coat covers tight navy scrubs filled with generous curves. She'd be beautiful if she didn't look like a green-eyed snake ready to bite.

"Dr. Steele?"

"Yes."

"I'm Sue, the lead nurse. I see you met Will."

"Yes."

"I'll take you to Medical."

"Thank you."

Emma drags her luggage and follows Sue, wondering what made her mad. Will follows them, his easy smile gone. They meander through miles of labyrinthic corridors flanked by identical numbered doors until Sue opens a hidden door to a steep set of metal stairs. She heads down, and Emma follows, struggling to carry her luggage down the stairs without breaking her neck. She's panting by the time Sue finally stops by a metal door marked Medical Office. The shelves by the entrance are loaded with brochures about STDs and open boxes of Tylenol, meclizine, and condoms.

"They're for the crew, so they don't need to ask, and they can help themselves even when we're closed. Come, I'll show you around. Will, I'll be with you in a minute."

Will nods and leaves through another unmarked door.

"Is he one of the nurses?" Emma asks.

Sue's lips tighten. "Not exactly. Will is my husband."

CHAPTER 2

The *Sea Horse's* Medical tour was more short than sweet. It started with Emma's new office, which turned out to have many functions. It was also the examination room, consisting of an ugly blue vinyl chair with retractable stirrups that looked like a torture table; the pharmacy, with glass cabinets that shelved all the ships' medications; and the secure drugs room, a locked steel cabinet where they kept controlled substances.

As if that weren't bad enough, Emma's office was also home to the slit lamp for eye exams, a massive metal contraption tethered to the wall so it didn't roll around on heavy seas; the autoclave where medical instruments got sterilized overnight, and the library — a dozen pathetic medical books, all older than Emma.

The one thing her office didn't have was a computer. Emma wondered how she'd keep records and do her research, but Sue's shrill voice interrupted her thoughts.

"It would be better if you didn't use perfume while you're here. Some patients are allergic, and we don't need any more work than we have."

Emma stared at her in disbelief. She never wore perfume. Then she remembered Gloria's broken bag and tried to explain, but Sue dismissed her with a flick of her hand. She pointed to the counter by the sink.

"This is where you count, cut, label, and package the pills."

"Me?"

Sue's smile would have made a snake proud.

"Who else? You're the doctor, aren't you?"

"But I'm not a pharmacist."

"Neither am I, dear. Nor is anyone else. You're a doctor; you should be able to count to ten and hand out a few pills," Sue huffed, heading to the waiting room.

The waiting room was an L-shaped hallway with a reception desk, a computer, and half a dozen chairs. Besides the two entries, one to the passengers' ship side and one to the crew's, it had a few more doors.

Sue opened the one labeled ICU.

"This is our resuscitation bay. There's the ventilator, the oxygen tanks, the critical care injections, and the intubating equipment. This is our only monitored room. Down the hall to the left is the storage room with canes, crutches, and walkers. Next to it is the X-ray room, then two isolation rooms. Those have nothing but a bed and a bathroom. That's where we quarantine noncritical patients."

Sue stomped from one door to another, dry-voicing Emma's many responsibilities and looking at her down her nose.

Her heart racing and her palms clammy with sweat, Emma smiled and nodded like it all made sense. But nothing did. She may be a doctor, but she's not a radiologist or pharmacist. Realizing that she's the doctor in charge of the three thousand souls on the ship but doesn't have a single consultant gave her the heebie-jeebies. On this boat, she's it. There's no cardiologist to fix heart attacks, no surgeon to check sick bellies, no GI to remove errant objects from tight orifices, and no orthopod to align broken bones. Emma is it. She's terrified, but it's too late to change her mind.

Sue opened the last unmarked door at the end of the waiting room.

"This is the door to our quarters. That one in the corner is your cabin. It's the only one that has a porthole. The stewards will bring you clean sheets and towels after they finish with the passengers, but they're too busy to clean our rooms. We do it ourselves.

"Make sure you carry your phone and pager at all times. And don't be late for the clinic. The passengers don't like it, and neither do I."

Sue turned around and disappeared, leaving Emma wondering what to do.

She checked her watch. She had fifteen minutes to get to Muster Station C, whatever that was, for the scheduled crew orientation. She'd better get moving.

CHAPTER 3

"Thanks for deciding to finally join us, doctor. My name is Lieutenant Degyter, and I will be conducting your new crew orientation."

The lieutenant glares at Emma above his thick wire-rimmed glasses, and the crowd of two-dozen crew clad in orange life jackets chuckles. Mortified, Emma bites her lip and squeezes behind Will's broad shoulders. No wonder she's late! First, she forgot her life jacket; then she got lost in the labyrinth of corridors and hidden stairs.

"We are gathered in the staff stairway at Muster Station C. A muster station is a place where the crew assembles before boarding a lifeboat. Your assigned muster station is printed on the tag affixed to your life jacket. In the event of a drill or an actual order to abandon ship, you will put on your life jackets and gather ONLY your necessary medications before proceeding to your assigned muster station for further instructions. Now follow me to the lower decks for the remainder of the crew orientation."

Chatting and laughing, the mixed crew shuffles behind him down a set of narrow metal stairs behind a hidden door, and Emma follows. They're the same people from the bus, but they're now in their uniforms. All but Will, and Gloria, whose lime-green pantsuit and orange hair make her look like an exotic parrot lost in a flock of boring ducks.

"You will notice that above the waterline, which is about Deck 3, the doors to the exterior are weathertight. They are designed to prevent the sea spray and the shallow deck ponding from entering the interior. Below decks, however, there are several heavy-duty watertight doors designed to prevent flooding from one compartment to another.

"Watertight doors operate automatically based on remote control from the Bridge. The power closing of the door is preceded by a flashing light followed thirty seconds later by a loud alarm horn as the door begins to operate. You may pass through the opening during the flashing light phase, but you may NOT enter the doorway when the alarm horn is sounding."

He pushes a button to demonstrate. Lights flash, then a blaring horn echoed by the metal walls blasts Emma's migraine into overdrive as the heavy doors slide closed into a watertight trap. There's something utterly final about the clack of metal against metal, and a shiver of dread runs down Emma's spine.

"I hope to never be here when these darn things are closing," Gloria mumbles, struggling to follow Emma and the others down the long hallway clomping on her eight-inch heels.

"How are you doing, doctor? Have you settled in?"

"I'm working on it," Emma says, remembering the luggage she left in the hallway and hoping no one steals her computer. The rest she can live without. She couldn't get into her cabin since it was locked, and the previous doc wasn't there.

"How about you? Have you…"

Lieutenant Degyter glowers at her, and she goes quiet.

"Fire suppression blankets and fire extinguishers are mounted throughout all the crew areas of the ship. Fire suppression blankets are used to smother small fires, such as a grease fire in a frying pan or a fire contained in a wastebasket. Fire extinguishers are used for larger fires.

"Overall, there are four common classes of fire extinguishers, although only two are used on board the *Sea Horse*. Class A extinguishers utilize pressurized water and are limited to use on ordinary combustibles such as paper, clothing and wood. They should not be used for electrical fires due to the risk of electrocution. Class A should also not be used on flammable liquids due to the danger of splashing. You'll recognize them by their spraying discharge nozzle, and the fact that they are marked with a big A. Got it, doctor?"

Emma nods, wondering what his problem is. She avoids even looking at Gloria for fear of being reprimanded again.

"But the most common type of fire extinguisher on the *Sea Horse* is the Class B-C extinguisher. Class B fires are flammable liquids, and Class C involves energized elements like electrical fires. The Class B-C extinguishers contain carbon dioxide under pressure so high that it is liquid in the tank. Once activated, the CO_2 expands to gas and high-velocity, dry-ice snow in the applicator horn. The horn should be directed at the base of the fire where the carbon dioxide displaces the oxygen necessary for combustion and extinguishes the flames."

"What a load! I sure hope I never need to use these things," Gloria whispers. "I already forgot which is which."

"Me too," Emma answers, wishing this whole stupid

thing was over so she could go to her cabin and take something for her headache. But the lieutenant is on a mission.

"There are a few fundamental rules about using CO_2 extinguishers. First, never grip the horn when directing the stream. Due to the expanding gas, it gets so cold it will freeze your hands. Second, remember that CO_2 displaces oxygen, so avoid using it in confined spaces. And finally, NEVER direct the extinguisher at a person due to the risk of suffocation and frostbite.

"Now we'll move on to the officers' club and crew mess areas..."

By the time Lieutenant Degyter dismisses them, Emma feels like she's been on the ship forever. She watches the crew disband and head in every direction, wondering where Medical is, disoriented after meandering through the ship's bowels for an hour.

"Where to next?" Will asks.

"Back to Medical, if I can find it."

"Come with me. I'm going there."

"Thanks," Emma says, grateful for his help but worried that seeing them together will get Sue's panties in a bunch again.

"You'll get used to Sue," Will says as if he can hear her thoughts. "She's a lovely woman, but these last few weeks stressed her terribly. She's been on edge ever since that nurse died. She and Nadja were best friends, you know."

"A nurse died? Here, on this ship?"

"Yes."

"How?"

Will shrugs. "I don't know; I wasn't here. Why don't you ask Sue? She'll tell you."

But seeing Sue's stormy face as she sees them enter

Medical, Emma doesn't dare ask anything. She grabs her luggage, scurries to her cabin, and knocks at the door.

CHAPTER 4

An hour later, Emma sits on her new bed on someone else's sheets staring through the dirty porthole at the gray concrete dock, wondering if leaving home to cruise the world was a good idea.

She quit her job as the medical director of a rural ER up north to look for adventure. She dreamed about amazing places, exotic foods, and interesting new people to bring some life to her life. But there doesn't seem to be any of that here.

The previous doc, a middle-aged man with a swelling midline and receding greasy hair, shook her hand and gave her a concise report.

"Not much happening."

He dropped the keys, the phone, and the pager on the desk under the porthole and grabbed his luggage.

"You'll be all right. Fajar, the crew doc, is OK. He's smart, fast, and smooth when he's not chasing some chick somewhere. The nurses aren't bad, especially Marico, who's a sweetheart, but watch out for Sue. She doesn't know her ass from a hole in the ground, but she thinks she's the cat's whiskers. And she's a viper, always ready to screw you over. I can't wait to see the last of her."

The heavy metal door slammed behind him like a prison gate. Emma studied her new home for the coming months and sighed. Not pretty. A ten-by-six-foot cabin bursting at the seams with overflowing garbage bins and an army of empty beer bottles under the desk. The bathroom, so small you had to sit on the toilet to pick something off the floor, smelled like a public urinal.

Emma sighed and closed the door, but the smell lingered, compounding the perfume on her fingers and making her nauseous. Seasick? But it can't be. They didn't even take off yet. She went to wash her hands for the fourth time as the pager went off.

1244. Medical, of course.

She called, but no one answered. She called again. Nothing. Oh well. She'd better. It's not a long walk.

Thirty seconds later, she's there, but there's no one else. She wonders what to do when a young Asian woman in navy scrubs comes in through the passenger entrance, followed by four crew members carrying a stretcher. The patient sitting up on the stretcher is bluish-gray. His heavy breath coming through pursed lips sounds like a locomotive pulling a train uphill.

"You're the new doc?" the woman asks. She's petite and beautiful, with narrow dark eyes, honey-colored skin, and straight hair so black it looks blue tied in a low ponytail.

"Yep."

"I'm Maria. I'm the first-call nurse today. Mr. Toki is short of breath. He just arrived. His wife said he stopped taking his meds so he didn't have to keep going to the bathroom on the plane."

"Really?"

Maria shrugs.

"They do that all the time. The first week on the ship is all about the travel: They either forgot their meds or stopped taking them; they gorge themselves at the buffet until they get sick. And they get seasick, of course. Things level out in the second week. You want an EKG?"

"Please. And labs."

Emma studies the patient. The blue man is neither young nor happy. He measures Emma with weary eyes and pushes away his oxygen mask. She pulls his hand away.

"Please don't do that. That mask helps you breathe, and it will help you feel better, OK? I'm Dr. Steele."

The man mumbles something in a language Emma doesn't understand, and one more thing dawns on her. Here, she's half a world away from her upstate ER. Just like her, her patients come from all over the world, and many don't speak English. And she has no translator.

Bummer. Emma sighs and listens to his lungs. He's got rales to his nipples. His lungs are overloaded with the fluid he's retained since he stopped his diuretic. But the oxygen did him good. He's still pale, but he no longer looks like a Smurf.

"Do you have any chest pain? *Douleur de poitrine? Dolor de pecho?*"

The man's eyes widen. He doesn't understand.

In a last-ditch effort, Emma strikes her chest with her fist and moans in pretend agony.

"Iye." The man shakes his head and laughs. Maria, who's working on an IV, laughs too.

"That was pretty good," she says. "There. This is his paperwork. He's Japanese."

Emma smiles, grateful that the patient came with instructions. He has no allergies. She checks his med list and decides to give him some sublingual nitroglycerin to open the blood flow to his heart and lower his blood pressure, and a touch of captopril to unload his lungs.

Just as the man starts to pink up, the door bursts open. All flushed, Sue blasts in, followed by a handsome Asian man in navy scrubs. She glances at the patient, then turns to Emma.

"Have you called yet?"

"Called who?"

"The hospital. You need to transfer him now. We're leaving in an hour."

"Why would we transfer him? He's fine. He responded to treatment."

Sue shakes her head.

"What if he gets worse? What if he gets in trouble on the crossing? Do you want to keep him in the ICU and watch him all night? I don't have the resources. I only have two nurses who work all day and are on call every other night. I can't have them watch somebody who has no business being aboard. If you call now, we can have the ambulance at the pier in half an hour."

"Then what?"

"Hopefully, he has travel insurance. The stewards will pack his stuff and drop it off. The shore representative will help with his travel arrangements when he's good to go and send him home."

"But he looks fine."

"I don't care. We can't start a five-week cruise with this. Fajar, you tell her."

The man behind her steps forward.

"Hi, doc. I'm Fajar, the crew doc. I've been on ships for five years. Sue's right. If we don't disembark him and he gets worse, he'll be a burden. And really, if he's unstable, he'd be better off staying here."

Emma's blood pounds her brain.

"Does he look unstable to you, Doctor?"

Fajar checks the man's vitals, looks at his EKG, and listens to his lungs.

"He doesn't."

"So, why should we disembark him?"

Fajar shrugs.

"How do you know he won't get worse?" Sue's voice, an octave too high, splits the air.

"I don't. But how do you know that any of the other three thousand passengers won't get worse? Should we disembark them all, just in case?"

"Listen, doctor. I know this is your first cruise, and you don't understand our situation. But, by the time you do, it will be too late. There won't be any place to drop him."

Emma sighs. "Sue, whose decision is to transfer patients?"

"Ours."

"Who signs the paperwork?"

"You do."

"I won't. Feel free to transfer him without me if you so choose. I am his doctor, and I think he'll be fine."

Sue's eyes burn holes in Emma, and her mouth zips into a line as she slams the door behind her.

Fajar shakes his head.

"I hope you're right, doctor. But if you don't mind my saying, you shouldn't make an enemy out of Sue, or she'll make your life miserable. You're better off having her as a friend."

He may be right, but it's too late. And there isn't much

Emma can do to please Sue. For whatever reason, Sue hated her guts from the moment she saw her, and Emma couldn't help but reciprocate. So that's that. Hopefully, the patient will do well and won't get her into more trouble than she's already in.

She rechecks his vitals, then turns to Maria.

"Give him some Lasix, please. I'll see him again in clinic this afternoon."

A steward wheels the patient back to his room, and Emma heads back to her cabin. In the hallway, she bumps into Fajar who ditched his scrubs for his officer's uniform and looks smashing.

He touches her shoulder with a dazzling smile.

"How about lunch, Doc? Let's go grab a bite and get acquainted."

CHAPTER 5

The Sea View Buffet on the *Sea Horse*'s ninth deck lives up to its name. Right now, its massive windows frame the curved Sydney Harbor Bridge arching like a black eyebrow above the glimmering blue sea. It's a breathtaking view, but Emma has a hard time focusing on the scenery as she squeezes through the entangled lines of passengers eyeing the buffet like they haven't seen food in months, even those who look like skipping a few meals would do them good. From toddlers to their grandparents, everyone elbows their way to the food-loaded stations, then carries their overloaded plates to their table with the satisfied grin of a successful Neanderthal hunter.

Emma is hungry — she always is — but the open display of gluttony gives her pause. Fajar sees her discomfiture and laughs.

"It's always like this on Day One. They'll start chilling in a day or two, but until then, you'd better eat early if you don't want to get trampled."

He takes her to a raised platform in the back where there's no view, but there are plenty of empty tables.

"This is the officers' area. It's usually full, but now they're all busy getting ready to sail. Let me get some coffee."

He combs his fingers through his long dark hair and slinks through the crowd with the effortless grace of a big cat. Minutes later, he's back with two steaming mugs of coffee smelling like instant.

"It's not the greatest, but I can use it after last night," he says.

"Me too," Emma says. She spent half the night talking a kid off the ledge on the Sidney Harbor Bridge. By the time she got him to come down, the night was over. She went to her hotel, packed, and left, hoping for a nap today. Fat chance!

She sips the dark, steamy liquid that tastes like dishwater and refrains from spitting it back. She's about to ask Fajar what he did last night, but he goes first.

"Good to have you here, Emma. Is this your first contract?

"Yes. I have a lot to learn. Tell me about the ship. And Medical."

"There's only five of us. You, me, Sue, Maria Conception, and Dana. Sadly, we lost Nadja not long ago."

"Nadja?"

"She was the third nurse. But in their infinite wisdom, the company decided that two nurses were enough for a ship with five thousand people, so they didn't replace her."

"What happened to her?"

Fajar looked down.

"She... She didn't make it."

"She didn't make it where?"

"She killed herself."

"Here, on the ship?"

Fajar nodded.

"How? And why?"

"Overdose. I think she overdosed on Fentanyl. Ever since that, the protocols have changed. We now need two people to open the lock to the controlled substances. Like that can stop someone from killing themselves! There are so many ways to do it, especially here on the ship. But let's speak about less terrible things. I was telling you about our team. Sue's the lead nurse, and she can be a little heavy-handed. She's not quite as smart as she thinks she is, so she compensates with extra leadership."

"I couldn't help but notice."

"You met Maria Conception. She's from Manila. Marico is actually a licensed physician, not a nurse, but the company didn't have an open crew doctor position on this cruise, so she took this contract as a nurse. She'll move on to take my place when my contract is over."

"When is that?"

"In Bangkok. Five more weeks, and I get to go home for a couple of months. I can't wait. I haven't seen my wife and kids in three months."

"That must be hard."

"It is, at times. Especially at night. But then, when I'm home, I have nothing to do but play with the kids for two months. And, thanks to my job, they can attend the best schools, and my wife doesn't have to work. To me, it's worth it. We'd struggle if I stayed home, even if I worked as a doctor."

"I see."

"It's pretty much the same with all the crew, you know. Unless their contract gets extended, they all work for four months, then go home for two.

"Then come back?"

"Sometimes. Unless their next contract is on another ship."

The buffet lines have thinned out, so they go get some food. The dozens of stations are loaded with more appealing dishes than Emma has ever seen in one place, and she wants to try them all: the chicken curry, the prime rib, the Caesar salad, and all the cheeses, breads, and desserts. She should know better, but she still overloads her plate, then feels bad about having judged the passengers for doing the same. Fajar, who got only got a salad and a roll, laughs at her.

"You too?"

Emma shrugs. That's why she hates all-you-can-eat buffets. It's impossible to hold yourself in check. And you can never ever work out enough to get rid of it, darn it.

"Tell me about our work. What do I do? What do you do?"

"You're responsible for the passengers. You have a clinic every morning and evening. They're supposed to be one hour, but they often run long, so you stay until you see everyone. And you must always be available for emergencies, so you carry your phone and pager no matter where you go."

"Why both?"

"Bad signal. The phone doesn't work everywhere on the ship, so you have the pager just in case."

Fajar takes a sip of his coffee. His eyes linger on Gloria, who's passing by. The girl smiles and waves, and Emma waves back.

"Who is she?" Fajar asks.

"The new singer."

"Pretty girl."

"Very. So what do you do?"

"I'm responsible for the crew. Fortunately, they're all young and healthy, so they mostly need preventive care. But truth be told, it's all hands on deck whenever things turn bad. We all do our best."

Emma takes a bite of the cold prime rib that looks way better than it tastes, wondering what he means by "when things turn bad" when her pager goes off. Medical, of course.

"There's a phone behind that column," Fajar says.

No answer. I may as well go see what it's about. I don't need all that food anyhow, Emma thinks. She heads to Medical, but she gets lost, of course. Fifteen minutes later, she's all out of breath when she opens the door to find Sue checking her Facebook at the nursing desk.

She greets Emma with a wide shark smile.

"So glad to see that you finally made it. Why don't we spend a moment establishing some ground rules?"

CHAPTER 6

Fajar picks at his salad watching Emma leave. *There's something about her*, he thinks. She's not that young — forties, maybe? Her hair's a mess, and that dirt-colored suit doesn't do much for her. Even a man can see she isn't trying. But there's something about her honest brown eyes and that easy smile that warms him inside.

"Like, really? She hasn't even unpacked yet, and you..."

Fajar laughs and shakes his head. "She's not my type, Dana. Come sit with me."

Dana sets her fruit plate on the table and pulls out a chair.

"That's BS, my friend. They're all your type. You've never seen a skirt you didn't get the urge to chase," she says, biting into a slice of blood-red melon.

"Not this one."

"Why not?"

"She's too much. Too old. Too stubborn. Too doctorly. I like my women soft, warm, and pliable."

"Really? So what were you doing in my bed last night, then?"

Fajar's eyes slide from Dana's laughing hazel eyes to her full lips, then to the curves that the navy officer uniform can't hide.

"Oh, you know. I couldn't resist. I can never resist you."

"Never?"

"Never."

"How about now?"

Fajar checks his watch. He has two hours before the afternoon clinic. He was planning to go to the gym, then catch a nap. But...

His finger traces Dana's wrist.

"I'll be down in ten."

CHAPTER 7

To the right, the famous Sydney Opera House blooms like a gleaming upside-down water lily emerging from the turquoise blue waters. Straight across the bow, the Harbor Bridge curves gracefully like a triumphant arch over the sparkling sea, so far ahead that the daredevils climbing it look like ants. To the left sits the whole spectacular Sydney Harbor, one of the most beautiful places on Earth.

The *Sea Horse's* departure from Sydney is a magnificent show that fills your soul with beauty, but Emma has no time to dawdle. She managed to steal a few minutes to watch the cast off, but now she's due for her clinic, though she can't imagine that anyone would choose to see her instead of enjoying the glorious views.

She snaps a couple more shots for Margret, her ex-mother-in-law and best friend, who travels vicariously with her through her pictures, then drags herself back to Medical, deep within the ship's bowels, wondering what new perversion Sue has in store.

But Medical is empty, thank goodness. Emma turns on

the computer to check her email, even though Sue already warned her that the desktop is for medical use only — while scrolling through Facebook. She told Emma to buy herself an internet card from the dispensing machines if she wanted the internet. She also assigned her a dozen engrossing courses on fascinating topics from waste management and fire awareness to cultural sensitivity to complete in her spare time.

They're still in port, but the ship's internet is slow as molasses. Emma taps her fingers, waiting for her email to download, when a slight, white-haired woman shuffles in through the passengers' entrance. She leans on a cane, and her narrow face is much lived in, but her ice-blue eyes sparkle with interest as she studies Emma.

"Are you the new doctor?" she asks in an accented voice.

"Yes, ma'am."

"What's your name?"

"I'm Dr. Steele."

"No. Your name."

"Emma."

"I'm Hanna. I live here."

"Here?"

"Yes. I live on the Horse."

Emma nods since she can't think of anything better to do.

"What can I help you with, Hanna?"

"Nothing yet. For now, it's the other way around. Let's sit and chat."

Emma closes her unopened mail and invites her to her new office. Hanna glances around.

"It's unchanged. You should make it more comfortable. Whoever thought that sitting with their back to the door was a good idea, I can't imagine. But it was like that even before the last idiot, the doctor before you."

Emma chokes with laughter. Hanna reminds her of her old friend Vera — fearless, outspoken, and wickedly funny.

"Where are you from, Emma?"

"Upstate New York."

"Really! I was born in Germany but lived in Buffalo for many years. Until my husband died."

"I'm sorry about your husband."

"Don't be. We're all better off with him gone. Even him. One day he had one too many beers and drove his lawn-mower off a bluff."

Emma looks for something to say. "You have children?"

"I used to."

There goes this safe subject.

"How come you live on the ship?"

"When my husband died, my son wanted to put me in a nursing home. He said I couldn't live by myself. That darn kid always thinks he knows everything! But I decided to see the world instead. I tried a few cruises and moved from one ship to the next until I discovered the Horse. That felt like home. So I sold my house and moved in. I have my own cabin, and I'm friends with most of the staff — except the new ones like you. Here, I get a room, board, entertainment, and travel for less than I'd live on at home. It's a good deal and great fun."

"Wow!"

"Wow, it is. I'm going on two years on the ship now. I know everything and everyone here."

"I wish I could say the same."

Hanna laughs. "No, you don't. But you will anyhow. How long are you here for?"

"Six months."

"First cruise?"

"Yes."

"Not married."

"Divorced."

"Good for you. I shouldn't have waited for the bastard to die. I could have started the good life sooner. Kids?"

"One girl."

"How old?"

"Eighteen."

"Phew. Kids are a pain in the ass until they reach twenty. Some stay that way."

Emma laughed.

"OK. Enough chit-chat. Let me tell you how everything works before the viper returns."

"The viper?"

"Sue, the lead nurse. What a venomous bitch! She hates doctors, so she makes their life miserable. Everyone's but Fajar's. Smart kid, he got himself in her good graces. Some say he warms her bed when Will isn't around, and she eats out of his hand. But he's the only one. The idiot who was here before you peed his pants whenever he saw her."

Emma's not that surprised. She can vouch that Sue takes some getting used to. But Fajar?

"Fajar? Really? He's got to be at least ten years younger than her."

"So what? The older the hen, the better the soup. Women get better with age. How old are you?"

"Forty-two."

"You'll soon be in your prime. Watch out for Fajar; he likes everything that wears a skirt, but not for long. He's a jumper, that one. I think Marico likes him too. She is not a bad girl, but she sucks up to Sue big time. Be careful what you say around her; she tells Sue everything. Then there's Dana. I haven't figured her out."

"I haven't met her yet."

"You will, soon enough. OK, Emma, it was good chatting with you, but I have to go. I must get ready for dinner with Captain Van Huis and his wife. He always wants me there on the first night to run interference. Passengers always eat and drink too much when they embark, then get obnoxious. Then they get seasick and get over it. You'll see that soon enough too."

Hanna stands with one shaky hand on her cane and the other on Emma's desk and straightens slowly. Emma watches her shuffle, worried that she's too unsteady to walk.

"How about I see you to your cabin? I have nothing better to do, and I'd love to see it."

Hanna's eyes turn to steel.

"I don't need help. And I've lived long enough to know when somebody's lying." Her voice softens, and she touches Emma's shoulder with a bony hand. "I know you mean well. But there's nothing more important to me than my independence. I'd rather die than depend on anyone."

She heads to the door and looks back.

"You're all right, Emma. I'll see you soon. But in the meantime, don't hesitate to drop by if you're in trouble."

CHAPTER 8

Trying to ignore the feeling of the walls closing around her in her bathroom, Emma struggles to get her hair into something that resembles a 'do, but the darn thing won't cooperate. And she's late, of course.

She gives up. She lets the mass of brown curls fall over her shoulders, brushes on some makeup to cover her shine, and glides on her Chocolate Dream lipstick. There. She's as good as she gets.

The invitation said "cocktail attire." Emma isn't quite sure what that means, but it doesn't matter. Thanks to all the books she packed, she only had room for one black dress and a pair of black flats, so that would have to do.

She reads it again.

"Captain Van Huis is pleased to invite you to the Sydney take-off cocktail party at 7 p.m. at the Ocean Bar. Champagne, cocktails, hors-d'oeuvres, live music, and enchanting company."

She'd shown the card to Marico.

"What's this?"

"That's the passengers' take-off party. It gives the women

an opportunity to show off their jewelry and assess the competition, and the men a chance to have free drinks. The point is getting everyone to meet new people and make some friends to enjoy the cruise, but it's awkward. They all stand around holding their glasses and pretending they don't have a care in the world until the waiters bring the hors-d'oeuvres trays. Then they all pounce like they haven't just gorged themselves at lunch and are about to do it again at dinner."

"Doesn't sound like much fun."

"It isn't. But it's your social obligation."

"Mine?"

"Sure. We, the nurses, are crew, so we're not invited. But you're the passenger doctor, so you're somewhere in between. You're not quite a passenger, but you're not crew, either. And they all want to meet the new doctor. You'll hear so many jokes about the Love Boat, you'll get sick. Not to mention when they start showing you their rashes. It all comes with the job. But the real party, the crew party, is tonight."

"Am I invited?"

"Of course. I'll take you there."

Marico was right, Emma thinks, standing by the wall in the Ocean Bar with a frozen smile on her face. She holds a frosty glass of something pink that tastes like mouthwash and pretends to listen to the band, but she's wondering when she can leave without being rude.

"Oh, there you are."

Dressed in a violet dress that sets off her blue eyes and wearing a sparkling necklace hiding her neck wrinkles, Hanna looks like she owns the place.

"Come, sit with me. I can't stand for long, and I fear

these people will crush my toes when they leap to grab the canapés."

Hanna finds an uncomfortably elegant loveseat by the wall. Emma sits beside her and watches the crowd, listening to Hanna's running commentary.

"You can't see the captain from here, but he's somewhere amongst that crowd. Like a queen bee, he can't take a step alone. He's not a bad guy, but he's a bit stiff. The best thing about him is his wife. Sadly, she won't be here since she doesn't care about mingling, but I'll introduce her to you one of these days. She's a hoot."

"See that tall blond guy in the white uniform? He's the first officer, and he does most of the work, but the passengers don't know it. The captain always gets the credit. That may be why he's so bitter. Or maybe because the cruise director ditched him. They had been together for months, and things were getting pretty serious, but suddenly, she gave him the boot. They say he didn't take it well."

"Who does?"

"The stewards. They're the ship's heart, and they know everything about everyone. How could they not? They always watch who's going where and with whom. They clean the rooms and take out the garbage; you wouldn't believe how much you can learn from someone's garbage. You'll know what they eat, how much they drink, and what they do when no one's watching, from pill bottles to used condoms. It's like the story of our lives, the garbage. I wish mine was more interesting than candy wrappers and used Q-tips."

"How do you know all that, Hanna?"

"My stewards are my best friends on the ship, and they love to gossip. Ask your steward if you ever need to know anything about anyone."

"I don't have one. We clean our own rooms."

"Really? Well, then, ask mine."

Hanna was a riot, and learning the ship's gossip was fascinating, but Emma sighed with relief when the party was over.

The crew party was something else. Marico led her along a labyrinth of narrow corridors deep inside the ship's belly, up and down metal stairs, until they reached a heavy door. It opened to a massive triangular space with a low bench around the bare metal walls. The place was chock-full of people and smelled like machine oil and heated bodies. A few scattered toolboxes and three cable drums turned into serving tables held platters overflowing with hors-d'oeuvres. Along the bare walls, buckets of ice were loaded with soft drinks and beer. A boom box screamed old-fashioned pop music that failed to cover the voices and the laughter. *There must be hundreds of people in here*, Emma thought.

"This is our secret party space. It's just at the ship's bow, and nobody ever uses it for anything but our parties. The officers wisely pretend they don't know about it. The crew needs to let off some steam after dealing with entitled passengers 24/7 and smiling until it hurts, even when they feel like blowing up. And it's better here than in the dining room."

A smiling man in a Hawaiian shirt brought them beers. Emma thanked him and took a sip, wishing it was wine instead. She set the bottle aside and watched the lively crowd. They were young, brown, and mostly men.

"Why so few women?" Emma asked.

"That's the makeup of the crew. The sailors, stewards, cooks, and waiters are all men. They work at sea for months, and they send home the money. Their women look after their children. There aren't many jobs for women on the ship — a few masseuses, estheticians, and entertainers. And a couple officers."

"That must make the women very popular."

"Of course. Even the ugly ones can afford to be picky. Why would they date a penniless sailor with a wife and kids at home? They'd rather have the officers, who are few, well-paid, and very popular," Marico said.

Emma leaned in to hear her above the ruckus.

"Won't somebody complain about the noise?" she asked.

Marico shook her head.

"We're by the engine rooms, deep in the ship's bowels. No one will hear a thing. Let's sit."

They sat on the cold metal shelf, sipping quietly on their beers. A couple started dancing, then another. The crowd receded to make room. Two more couples followed, and Emma recognized Fajar, dancing cheek-to-cheek with a stunning blonde.

"Who's that?"

"The cruise director."

"Are they..."

"Who knows? And who cares? Wanna dance?"

"Why not?"

They joined the other dancers, who welcomed them with bright smiles. The eighties hits reminded Emma of her youth, and she gave in to the rhythm. She danced and laughed and let herself enjoy the party and the people. She'd never met them until that morning, but they were now her team. And for the first time in forever, she felt like she belonged.

CHAPTER 9

When a cacophony of noises wakes her up, Emma can't remember where she is. She feels for Guinness's comforting touch by the bed, but the dog is missing.

She fumbles with the light and discovers that she's in a cell no larger than an elevator. The porthole to liquid darkness tells her that she's on a ship, and she remembers. She left her home, her job, and her life to escape her black cloud, see the world, and grow. She left her daughter Taylor, baby Hope, Victor, and even her beloved German shepherd Guinness, and she hasn't heard from them in days since she still didn't get her mail.

But there's no time for that now. The phone rings, and the pager beeps again. Emma pulls on her white coat over the navy scrubs she slept in, grabs the black doctor's bag she never leaves behind, and blows through the door to Medical. Fortunately, it's only a fifty-foot commute from her bed to her office.

Beyond the quiet, dark hallway to their cabins, Medical is hopping big time. Bright cold lights spill over a haggard

Marico holding a phone to each ear. A patient on a stretcher lies in the middle of the floor as a nurse leans over to assess him. Two crew members rush in with a second stretcher, carrying a woman who looks like she's fixing to die.

"What's going on?" Emma asks.

"Hi, Doctor. I'm Dana. We've had five calls for sick people this evening. These are just the first two. Another stretcher team is bringing more, but we're running out of rooms and stretchers. These two complain of trouble breathing and burning eyes," says the unknown nurse.

Five people at the same time? Inhalation injury, maybe? Some sort of fumes that burned their lungs and eyes? Emma kneels on the floor to listen to the man's lungs. They're junky, but he's moving air. She looks into his tearful eyes. He's elderly — but then, so is everyone on this darn ship. His red eyes with pinpoint pupils are scared. His shaky hands grab Emma's.

"Don't let me die, please. Don't let me die."

Emma holds his hand.

"Of course not. Can you imagine the amount of paper-work I'd have to do? And we'd have to put you in a refrigerator, and we can't. They're all full of food since we just embarked."

The man starts laughing through his tears, then breaks into a cough. Emma glances at his vitals and checks his pulse. It's slow but strong, and he looks OK. She orders a breathing treatment and goes to check on the woman.

Marico hangs up both phones and stares at Emma with terrified eyes.

"I've never seen something like this. It's like they got poisoned or something. All of a sudden, all these people get sick. I have two more cabins that need transport."

"Cabins?"

"Yes. Both passengers in the cabin got sick, just like these two."

"Which cabins? Are they close to each other?"

Marico checks her notes.

"632 and 634. These two are from 638."

"How about 636?"

Marico gawks at her like she's grown a third ear.

"No."

"Call 636. If there's no answer, send somebody there now."

Marico picks up the phone as Emma checks the woman. Her eyes are wide with fear, and her pupils are tiny black holes. Pinpoint pupils again. Opioids, maybe? But then, why the junky lungs? The woman's crepey skin is hot and dry, and she wheezes up a storm.

Emma turns to Dana.

"Let's check her temperature, please. And give her a breathing treatment too."

She turns back to the man, but the woman grabs her hand.

"Thank you. Thank you. Please do whatever it takes to keep my husband alive. I've got cancer already; I don't have much left, but please do whatever you can for him."

"I'll do my best for you both, but you look fine. We'll move you to a side room to make room for the others to come. It'll be a little tight."

The stewards move them to an isolation cabin to make room. Minutes later, four more stretchers clog the waiting room, making Medical look like M*A*S*H. The waiting room chokes with stretchers and crying patients coughing and asking for help. The stretcher teams step out to make room, but they stand by the door, waiting for orders.

"Let's make some room. Move these two to the ICU and those two to my office," Emma says, just as a sweaty Fajar barges in, dressed in a skimpy pair of tight shorts and a sleeveless T-shirt.

"What the heck?"

"My thoughts precisely. And more are coming. Can you check on those two?"

Fajar heads to the ICU, and Emma turns to Marico.

"Did you get through to room 636?"

"I've tried again and again, but there's no answer."

Emma's heart goes cold as a wave of hot blood rushes to the top of her head. *Why the heck can't people ever follow instructions?*

She takes a deep breath and looks straight into Marico's frightened eyes.

"SEND SOMEBODY TO BREAK DOWN THE DOOR. NOW."

"But..."

"Never mind. Come with me."

Emma grabs her doctor's bag as Marico takes the heavy Red Cross bag with the Bright Star equipment. They blow through the stewards that block the door to take the crew stairs to the sixth deck. But, unlike the wide, carpeted passenger stairs, these metal steps are steep and narrow, like a fire escape. Emma's about to be sick by the time she gets to the sixth deck. She stops for a moment to breathe, then heads down the mile-long hallway flanked by dozens of identical doors to look for 636.

When she finally finds it, she rings the doorbell, knocks at the door, then rings the doorbell again.

Nothing.

"The universal key," Marico says.

Emma remembers that the Security folks gave her an emergency card programmed to open any door on the ship. She slides it through, and the lock clicks.

Emma sighs and pushes the heavy door, hoping from the bottom of her heart that she's not about to interrupt two old people who took off their hearing aids to have kinky sex.

CHAPTER 10

No such luck. Nothing moves in the darkness heavy with ominous silence. Emma flips on the switch, flooding the narrow inside cabin in cold bright light, and gasps.

The place is so cluttered it's oppressive, reminding Emma of when she got stuck in a cave in Belize many years ago. Like then, she feels the walls closing in on her as her claustrophobia takes over. Emma hates closed spaces, and every instinct tells her to blast out the door. But she can't.

She takes a few deep breaths to slow down her heart as her eyes sweep over the piles of stuff. Clothes everywhere. Toiletries, magazines, dirty dishes, and pill bottles pile upon each other, making the room look even smaller. The only big thing in the room is the bed, where two old people curl back-to-back, each under their own blanket, looking asleep.

Emma leans over the tiny white-haired woman, grabs her shoulder, and shakes her. The woman opens her eyes and mumbles something, and Emma's heart floods with relief. The woman's pulse is slow, and her skin burns, but she's breathing. She wheezes, and her chest heaves with every breath, but she's very much alive.

Emma glances back. Marico and the stretcher team are waiting at the door.

"Take her to Medical. Get her vitals, give her a couple of breathing treatments, and get labs, blood, and urine. Toxicology and carbon monoxide, please. And send me another stretcher team."

She moves to the man on the other side of the bed. He looks asleep, but shaking him won't wake him up. Oh well. Emma buries her knuckles in his chest in a rough sternal rub. He moans and pushes her away, and Emma sighs with relief. She gently pulls up his eyelids to check his pupils. They're pinpoint, and his heart is way too slow.

She slips an oxygen mask on his face and checks his vitals. His oxygen is so-so, but the blood pressure's not bad, everything considered. A carbon monoxide monitor would come in handy right now, Emma thinks, looking for a window to open. But there's none. Room 636 is one of the cheap windowless inside cabins, so she grabs a chair and props the door open instead.

As she waits for the stretcher, Emma checks the pill bottles on the table. There's a basket full of them: blood pressure pills, diabetes pills, urinary retention pills, dementia pills. Her eyebrows raise as she sees the OxyContin. That might be why he won't wake up. Or it may not.

Like most ER doctors, Emma doesn't believe in coincidences. All these cabins next to each other full of people with similar symptoms? There's got to be something about the place. But what? The ventilation, maybe?

She's still looking for the aircon vents when the stretcher team arrives to take the patient down to Medical, and Emma follows. He's the sickest, so he gets the ICU bed. Fajar, sweaty but as handsome as ever, takes over his care to free Emma to see the other patients.

"Thanks, Fajar. You know what? Let's make him naked and decon him."

"Decontaminate him? But why?"

"I've got a bad feeling. All these people in neighboring cabins with the same symptoms smell like some sort of environmental exposure."

"To what?"

"I don't know. Some sort of fumes? Carbon monoxide? If I had to guess, I'd say they're cholinergic. I know the symptoms don't totally jive, but that's the best I can come up with."

Fajar's eyes grow wide.

"Really? How could that be?"

"I don't know. Maybe they had bedbugs or cockroaches and fumigated those cabins before the trip. Or rats and they spread poison? I don't have a good explanation, but in the spirit of Occam's razor, we need to find a single unifying explanation for all these people getting sick simultaneously. It may be something in the food or the water, but if I had my guess, I'd say it's some exposure."

"But you said this guy is on opiates. That could explain his symptoms."

"Some, but not all. And how about the others?"

Fajar shrugs. "Still, let's give him some Narcan and see what happens. If he responds, we'll know it's the opioids."

"I wouldn't do that if I were you. He's a chronic user, so he'll go into acute withdrawal and become an absolute pain. And you still won't exclude an exposure. I advise against it as long as he maintains his airway and breathes. Either way, please get him decontaminated."

Emma leaves the ICU to check on the woman. Her lungs sound better after the breathing treatments, and she's more with it. She's clearly heading in the right direction, so Emma smiles at Marico, who's working on an IV.

"Good job, Marico. Thank you."

Marico shrugs but doesn't answer.

What's up with her? Is she miffed that I told her what to do? But that's my job, Emma thinks, just as an earth-shattering scream coming from the ICU shakes the walls. Everyone freezes.

Emma sighs and walks in to see Fajar fighting with the unconscious patient who's now very much alive. Fajar struggles to keep him on the stretcher, but the sleepy old man has turned into a screaming monster who pulls on his lines and tries to punch Fajar.

"Let me go! Let me go!"

The stewards rush in to help, but it's too late. The man's IV catheter broke. A geyser of blood spurts to the ceiling, spraying Fajar, Emma, and everyone else. The old man flails, bites, and screams obscenities as three men struggle to hold him down.

"Welcome to the miracle of acute opioid withdrawal," Emma says, grabbing his arm to put pressure on the bleeding site.

Fajar wipes the blood off his face with the back of his hand. His eyes are stormy, and his mouth zipped into a thin line.

"What do I do now?"

Emma shrugs. "Go take a shower. There isn't much we can do. We'll just have to keep him safe and wait it out."

Oh, how she'd love to say, "I told you so." Fortunately, she knows better.

CHAPTER 11

Overlooking miles and miles of blue ocean, the captain's office up high on the navigation deck is meant to impress. The ancient maps hanging on the dark sienna walls are framed works of art. A brass compass and an antique sextant hold down the piles of papers on the mahogany desk. That desk alone is as big as our whole ICU, Emma thinks, looking up from the low chair she was offered and wondering about the ship's priorities.

Looming over his desk and decked in the full bling of his naval uniform, the captain is tall, blond, and skinny as a poplar in November. And just about as happy. The bright windows frame his silhouette and leave his face in the shade as he looks down at Emma. She squints, wishing she could look into his eyes. But that's not how interrogations are performed, is it?

Emma is in trouble, and she knows it. She just doesn't know why. She's been wondering since his phone call pulled her out of her morning clinic. Not a bad thing, mind you, even though she scurried out through the waiting room, trying to ignore a dozen eyes burning into her back.

The captain snorts.

"Dr. Steele. It has come to my knowledge that you have been spreading rumors about some strange exposure making my passengers sick. Please explain yourself."

His icy voice is almost unaccented, and his tone is firm.

That's got to be Sue, Emma thinks. Emma voiced her suspicions to Fajar, who told Sue, and now she's in deep doo-doo. But then, what's new?

"Sir, I..."

"Captain Pieter van Huis."

"Captain Van Huis, we have eight passengers with similar symptoms whose cabins are all next to each other. You think that's normal?"

"What symptoms?"

"Wheezing. Abdominal discomfort. Slow heart rate. Small pupils."

The captain watches and waits, but Emma can wait him out. She's been doing it with patients, families, and consultants for twenty years. She knows the best way to teach people is to listen to them. The less you speak, the more they listen.

"What else?"

"I'm not sure yet. But what we do have makes me think about toxic exposure."

"What kind?"

"Some toxic fumes? Maybe pesticides? Do you have anything like that on the ship?"

"I'm the one who asks the questions here."

Emma shrugs. *Fine. Be that way.*

"How are the passengers doing?"

"They're better. But they shouldn't return to their cabins before they get decontaminated and checked. Whatever made them sick before might make them sick again. And could you have somebody check the ventilation system? Or whatever other systems these four cabins share? Unless maybe a gas that went in under the door..."

"Dr. Steele, this is a cruise ship. Nothing goes under the doors. They're watertight."

"The water bottles? The shampoo? The mini-bar? Maybe there was a batch of a contaminated product that got to these particular four cabins?"

"Why?"

"By mistake? Or with criminal intent? Do they share the same steward? Maybe they're all friends and had dinner together?"

"You have an awe-inspiring imagination, Dr. Steele. You would do well to keep it in check. The same with sharing information. Do you know what will happen if three thousand passengers hear a rumor that somebody's trying to poison them? Have you ever been in an unrest, Dr. Steele?"

"No."

"I have. If somebody catches a drift of your... highly unusual ideas, they'll share them with their friends, who will share them with other friends. Before dinner, we'll have a mutiny on our hands. I will, in fact, while you'll be sitting pretty in Medical, distributing cough lozenges. And, unlike your cockamamie ideas, this is a fact. Then somebody will put this out on Facebook or Twitter for the world to know, and we'll get stranded. No port will allow us to disembark before ensuring we don't carry some God-awful contagious disease that could start a pandemic. We'll be quarantined at sea for God knows how long. All that because you can't keep your mouth shut."

The captain leaves his chair to pace around the room.

"Do us both a favor. Next time something like this

crosses your mind, don't tell anyone but me. Not the crew doc, not the lead nurse, not even your toothbrush. Tell me."

"Are you going to do something about those four rooms?"

"I already have. The engineers started checking them this morning. When they're done, everything inside will be sanitized or replaced. Your patients have been upgraded to outside cabins and separated. And no, they didn't have dinner together. I checked. Three different stewards are looking after those four rooms. As you can see, your wild scenarios are completely unfounded."

So he dismissed her ideas, but he'd been thinking along the same lines even before she spoke to him. He understands that this whole thing makes no sense, but he doesn't want the rumor to spread.

"That's it. Please take care of your patients and leave the rest to me. And do not, I repeat, do not share your suspicions with anyone."

Emma heads to the door.

"Dr. Steele?"

"Captain?"

"Stay vigilant and come to me should anything untoward happen again."

CHAPTER 12

Thus dismissed, Emma takes the metal back stairs two at a time. It's been half an hour since she left her morning clinic to see the captain, leaving behind a waiting room full of passengers. They didn't like it. Nor did the nurses, who had to keep them happy when she left.

Emma's sweating and puffing like a locomotive by the time she blasts through the door to Medical. Still, the waiting room is empty but for Dana, who greets her with a smile.

"No rush. Nobody's dying. Have yourself some coffee."

"Where's everybody?"

"I sent them to their cabins. I told them the captain called you for an emergency, and I'll call them back when you return. They never grumble when you mention the captain, and they'll be happier up there than down here with me. Me too."

Emma laughed.

"Thank you, Dana. I owe you one."

"You owe me nothing. That's what we do."

The Medical kitchen is barely large enough to turn around. Still, it has a microwave and a coffeemaker for late-night emergencies. Emma makes coffee and brings a mug to Dana, who's working the phone calling people back.

"Most are too busy to come back. One would wonder what they're busy with, but never mind. They'll be in this afternoon or tomorrow."

"Thanks."

They sip on their coffees in easy companionship. Emma's shoulders soften, and she relaxes for the first time since last night's disaster.

"Where are you from, Dana?"

"I'm from Romania. Transylvania, to be precise."

"Transylvania? I thought that only existed in Bram Stoker's imagination."

"No, it's real, all right. Bram Stoker just borrowed it."

Emma smiles.

"Is Dracula real too?"

"Not anymore. But he's borrowed, too, from Vlad Țepeș, Vlad the Impaler, a fifteenth-century Wallachian prince who loved blood. Brașov, my hometown, is just a few miles from Bran Castle, where Dracula is supposed to have lived. He didn't, but it makes for great marketing."

Dana smiles, but her kind hazel eyes are worried.

"How are you doing, Doctor?"

"I'm OK, thanks, but there's so much I need to learn. Nothing here is like my old ER. And everything takes some time to get used to. I just hope I don't kill anyone while I'm learning."

Dana laughed.

"You won't. Sick people are sick people, no matter where you are. And the rest is just details. And we're all here to help."

"Thanks. Please let me know if you catch me doing something wrong."

"You mean it?"

"Of course."

"Then I'll tell you. Beware of Sue. She doesn't like to be challenged, and she can make your life miserable."

"She already has."

"You haven't seen anything yet. And it's not just you. Your patients will suffer too. Avoid irritating her, and remember that she responds well to flattery. Everybody walks on eggshells around her, even Will."

"I haven't seen Will ever since I arrived. What happened to him?"

Dana laughs.

"You only embarked yesterday, remember? I bet it feels like you've been here forever. He's doing his thing, as usual."

"Does he work on the boat?"

"No. As Sue's husband, he gets to cruise for free. But he likes to keep himself busy and stay out of her hair. He spends his time helping the folks at the shore excursion office. They're grateful and slip him a free shore excursion whenever they can."

"He looks like a nice guy."

"He is. But don't get too close to him. Sue won't like it."

"Sue doesn't seem to like a lot of things."

Dana laughs.

"You catch on quickly, don't you? Sue knows what she wants and won't stop at anything to get it. Be careful and watch your back. She..."

The door opens to let in a steward pushing a wheelchair with an elderly gentleman covered in blood. The fragile, white-haired woman following him wavers like she's ready to fall.

Emma helps her to a chair as Dana moves the patient to a stretcher.

"What happened?"

The woman's trembling lips struggle to form words that won't come.

"He fell."

"How?"

"He slipped on the wet deck and struck his head against a chair."

"Is he taking any blood thinners?"

"Yes."

"Which?"

The woman shrugs.

"What is he taking them for?"

"His diabetes."

I don't think so, Emma thinks. *Unless his doctor attended some online medical school.*

The patient holds a bloody towel to his head, but a steady stream of blood runs down his forehead into his eyes, then drips from his chin to the floor. Emma grabs a two-by-two piece of gauze. She removes the towel, and a geyser of blood spurts from the three-inch gash in his scalp, splashing her, before she puts her finger on the bleeder.

"How do you feel, sir?"

"OK." The man nods.

"Don't move your head, please. Does your neck hurt?"

Emma palpates his spine with her free hand, checking each vertebra for tenderness and watching for a grimace indicating pain.

"No."

"Does anything else hurt?"

"No."

Emma turns to Dana.

"Get me some lidocaine with Epi, please. A 10cc syringe and two needles: #18 and #27."

She blindly injects the lidocaine under the gauze to numb him up and slow the bleeding, then turns to his weary wife.

"We'll take care of the wound. A few staples or stitches should take care of the external bleeding. The more challenging part is ensuring there's no bleeding in his brain."

"How will you do that?"

I'll be damned if I know, Emma thinks. *If I were home, he'd be in the CT scanner already. And even if everything looked great, I'd still rescan him in a few hours. But here? I have no CT. I'm lucky if I can get an X-ray, which is useless for this.*

She turns to Dana, who's working on getting labs.

"When's the next port? And where?"

"Whitsunday Island in two days."

"Do they have a hospital there?"

"Not much."

Emma sighs. In two days, it won't much matter anyhow. By then, he'll be either out of danger or dead.

"I need to know his medications. Can you get me the list, please?"

The steward takes the woman to her cabin as Emma cleans the wound and starts stitching, but it's slow going. The Epi helped, and the bleeder is no longer spurting, but there's still enough ooze to drown her field of view. Oh well. It is what it is. It may not look pretty, but so what? Nobody'll see it under the hair. The real problem is whether he's bleeding in his brain.

"Dana, how can we transfer him out?"

"By helicopter. But it's hard to do unless they're in extremis. It's also costly unless they have travel insurance. Do you have medical travel insurance, sir?"

"I have Medicare."

"No travel insurance?"

"No."

Dana shakes her head.

"That's no good. If we get a helicopter to take him ashore, they'll slap him with a bill not many can afford. And we'll cut his cruise short, possibly for nothing."

Emma sighs. *The story of my life. Never enough data to make an informed decision. You always have to go blind.*

"Let's watch him for now. We'll talk about transfer if he gets worse." She turns to the patient.

"Sir, I'll see you back here this afternoon at four to see how you're doing."

She watches the steward pushing him out with a tight heart. She hopes she did the right thing, but in her line of business, you never know.

CHAPTER 13

By the time morning clinic is over, Emma is two hours late, and her back is killing her. She's also starving, since after last night's debacle, she slept in and missed breakfast, but she's so exhausted she decides to skip lunch for a nap. *It won't hurt me to lose a pound or two,* she thinks, as she struggles to lock her office.

The crew door opens, and Marico steps in. After being on the first call yesterday, she's off today, and she looks gorgeous in her pink sundress. Emma, still in the wrinkled scrubs she wore to sleep last night, feels dirty and old next to her.

"How about lunch? Has anyone shown you the crew dining room?" Marico asks.

"I didn't know there was one."

"Of course, there is. That's where the crew eats. We, in Medical, can go up to the dining room as long as we dress up. The crew can't. But they have their own kitchen, and the cafeteria serves their favorite comfort foods. You'll love it."

Emma isn't so sure, but she's hungry. And she can't miss

an opportunity to learn about the ship and a chance to make a friend. She may get half an hour before the afternoon clinic to lie down and rest her back with some luck. And if not, that's what Motrin is for. She follows Marico along the brightly lit steel corridors of the third deck, deep inside the ship's bowels, taking it all in.

"Passengers don't come down here. That's why the crew can feel at home," Marico says.

She's right. Unlike up on the passengers' decks, where the crew is only concerned with the guests' comfort, down here, they come alive. Laughing sailors in soiled uniforms, their nails dark with dirt, slap each other's backs. Sharply dressed in their forest-green uniforms, three stewards give a wide berth to the harried navy-clad officers zooming between their offices. A trio of graceful tall blondes — dancers or yoga instructors? — stop to check the posting board that advertises crew-only shore excursions, ping-pong tournaments, and crew parties. A gray-haired woman looking like a hung-over psychic buys internet cards from the automatic dispenser on the wall. Emma wonders what she's doing on the ship.

This whole new world is so unlike the passengers' side of the *Sea Horse* that it's hard to believe it's the same ship, and Emma has to struggle not to gawk.

The crew cafeteria is way down the hallway. It's sparsely furnished, as bright as an OR, and just as friendly. A long stainless-steel counter stretches along the side wall, leaving room for a dozen melamine tables surrounded by colorful chairs. A few sailors, all men, eat and chat in a melodious language. They glance at them but look away when Emma catches their eye.

Marico grabs a tray and gets in line. Emma follows.

"There's always at least one Indonesian and one Filipino dish, so everyone can have their comfort food since the crew is half Indonesian and half Filipino. There's also food from the upstairs kitchens, and there's always a soup, rice, fruit, and a salad bar."

"Is the crew always like that?"

"Yes. They're both less expensive than hiring Americans or Europeans. And most Filipinos speak English, so they work as stewards and waiters. The Indonesians are mostly sailors and cooks. The entertainers are often Eastern European, the officers are South African and Dutch, the trainers are South American, and the performers are from all over the world. There's a lot of cross-over, of course, but we can truly call ourselves a global crew."

Marico uncovers the first pot and smiles.

"Fish heads! I love fish head curry." She fills her plate with rice and curry and finds an empty table.

Emma sighs. She may be hungry, but she's not feeling up for fish heads today. She hesitates between something brown that may be cabbage sprinkled with scattered bits of shiny fat, and pieces of overcooked chicken drowning in a thick red sauce. Oh well. She pours some red sauce over her rice, adds a few chicken shreds, and sits across from Marico, trying to find something nice to say.

"What an interesting place."

"It is, isn't it? The food's always great. And eating here saves time since you don't need to change and rush to the Sea View and back. Plus, you don't have to worry about passengers showing you their rashes between the salad station and dessert."

Emma laughs. To her surprise, the hot panang curry bursts with flavor, and it's so hot it brings tears to her eyes.

This is the best lunch she's had in ages. Her week in Sydney was phenomenal. She toured the Opera House, zoomed across the Sydney Harbor in the shaggy Manley Ferry, and watched the Tasmanian Devils fight over carcasses at the Sydney Zoo, but as for the cuisine? Their best dish is beer, and Emma doesn't even like beer.

Marico's kind eyes watch Emma with concern.

"How are you doing, Doctor? You look tired. No wonder, with the night we had. I can't remember another one like that, and I've been working on ships for years. And it was your first night on the ship. I don't know how you did it, but you performed like a pro."

"Call me Emma, please. Only thanks to you and the team. You have such a strong team."

"We do have a good team. Sue can be rough, but she's a good team leader. Dana is hard-working and bright. And Fajar is a great doctor."

"He's not hard on the eyes, either."

Marico smiled.

"So I've heard, but he's not my type. How about you? Are you married? Kids?"

"I'm divorced, and I have an eighteen-year-old daughter who just had a baby. You?"

"I also have a daughter. I was just sixteen when I had her. I was young and foolish, and that baby could have been the end of my future. But my parents took care of us both. They adopted her, and they sent me to medical school. I couldn't be more grateful. Now it's my turn to take care of them."

"How old is your daughter?"

"She's sixteen, but I hope she's wiser than I was at her age. There. This is her."

Marico scrolls through her phone to show Emma a

smiling Asian girl with warm honey skin and almond-shaped eyes.

"Wow. What a beautiful girl! And she looks just like you. It must have been hard to leave her behind."

"Yes. But my parents are her parents. She's happy and well cared for."

"Wonderful."

Emma remembers Taylor, and her heart tightens. Unlike Marico, she didn't exactly leave her daughter in the arms of a loving family. She left her struggling with a new baby and college and trying to figure out her life. She's not alone, of course — her father's there. So are her grandma and her friends. But Emma doesn't feel proud of it.

It was the right thing to do. Taylor needs room to grow a conscience, and having Emma there made it hard. Still, she wishes she was a better mother. She loves Taylor, but not with the kind of unconditional love mothers are supposed to have for their children. She's not blind to Taylor's flaws. *That girl needs to grow up,* Emma thinks, remembering the lives Taylor already managed to wreck.

Marico picks a fish head with her fingers and disassembles it with the smooth moves of a clockmaker.

"What do you think was wrong with the patients the other night?"

Emma remembers the captain's words: "You care for your patients and leave the rest to me. And don't share your suspicions with anyone."

"I... I'm not sure. A virus? Food poisoning, maybe?"

"Food poisoning?"

Marico's delicate eyebrows rise in surprise, and Emma feels like an idiot. Of course, it's not food poisoning, and they both know it. She shrugs.

"Sorry, Marico, that's BS. I'm just making this up. I honestly don't know. What do you think?"

Marico glances around to make sure nobody's listening.

"I think somebody tried to poison cabin 636. The others were just collateral damage."

CHAPTER 14

After throwing that bomb, Marico goes back to her fish head. She sucks dry every bone, then sets them on the edge of her plate in an artful arrangement.

Her mouth agape, Emma stares at her, wondering if she's heard her right. The hot curry drips on her chin, and she wipes it off, watching Marico savor her food.

"I'm sorry, you said?"

"Somebody poisoned 636. The rest were just collateral damage."

"But why?"

"You know who the folks in 636 are?"

"No."

"They are the cruise director's parents. I wonder who tried to get rid of them. And why."

Emma stares at her, wondering if the girl has lost her mind. Unperturbed, Marico pushes away her plate, empty but for the neatly arranged fish bones, and moves on to her chocolate ice cream.

"This isn't bad, but the coconut is even better. The green tea too. Did you try it?"

"Why would anyone want to kill the cruise director's parents?"

"Good question. That's kind of rude, isn't it? After all, they're just a couple of demented old people who aren't doing any harm. Why kill them? Unless they want to hurt their daughter and decided to kill them to get to her."

Emma feels a migraine coming. She pushes her plate aside.

"But who would want to hurt the cruise director? And why?"

"Take your pick. There's a long line. Some say Amanda slept her way up to the top. Just a few years ago, she started as a singer. Now she's got the third highest job on the ship after the captain and the hotel director. Who knows how many toes she stepped on to get there? Some important people, too. She was dating the first officer and ditched him a couple of months ago. He's mad as hell. Did you meet her?"

"Not yet."

"You will. I can't wait to see what you think. But, of course, there's also the opposite possibility.

"Which is that?"

"The old folks, they're both demented. They need a lot of care, and they're a burden. She brought them aboard rather than hire someone to care for them at home since it was cheaper. But they're a major inconvenience since they need a lot of work. She'd be free if it wasn't for them."

"Are you saying..."

"I'm saying I don't know. Maybe somebody tried to hurt Amanda, or somebody tried to do her a favor. Or, more likely, she did it herself."

The enormity of the accusation leaves Emma speechless. Killing one's parents? That's terrible. She never loved her mother, but killing her? The idea makes her shiver.

"What... what makes you think she'd poison them?"

"Did you notice the scent in the room when we got there last night?"

Emma tries to remember. Opening the door to the darkness. The room smelled like old people, urine, and old bodies that needed a bath. And maybe... maybe something else? Something sweet. Like pipe tobacco?

"Not really."

"It's Red Door, her perfume. She'd just been there."

"But that doesn't mean she was poisoning them! They're her parents; of course, she visits them."

"In the middle of the night? And then she left them there, sick, without telling anyone?"

"Maybe she visited earlier, and the perfume lingered. Or maybe she lent her perfume to her mother."

"Her mother didn't smell like perfume. I took her down to Medical, so I know. But you know what? You may be right. After all, I barely know her, and the fact that she's a cast-iron bitch doesn't necessarily mean she'd kill her parents. How about some dessert?"

Emma would like to pursue this, but Marico will have none of it. She chats about the weather and the upcoming port like nothing happened, leaving Emma with a deep unease.

CHAPTER 15

Emma lies in her cabin to rest her back, wondering about Marico. Can the girl be off her rocker? She's charming and sounds reasonable, but what she said is hard to fathom. And why would she tell all this to Emma, a complete stranger?

On the other hand, Emma is the passengers' doctor, in charge of their health and well-being. Hence, it is Marico's responsibility to share any relevant information. And as yet, there's no reasonable explanation for what happened last night. It's highly improbable that anyone would poison two harmless elderly people, least of all their daughter. But it wouldn't be the first time that reality turned out stranger than fiction.

Emma sighs and gets up. She's too wired to rest, so she decides to refresh herself on the finer details of environmental exposures. After all, it's been years since she studied toxicology.

Glad that Medical is still closed for lunch, she turns on the office computer. But the darn thing belongs in a museum rather than a modern medical office, so it takes forever to warm up. When it finally does, the internet-at-sea is slower than a drunk snail. Emma curses under her breath and taps her foot as she waits for her favorite medical database to upload.

She studies the L-shaped waiting room, which is really just a hallway to her exam room, Fajar's office, and the ICU. An unmarked door opens to their cabins at the long end of the L.

It's nice to have a short commute, Emma thinks, *but parading through the waiting room every time you come and go is not. Especially if you're dressed for the gym or the pool.* Not that she got to go there, but someday she might.

The computer clicks. Emma is finally in business. She starts researching toxins and poisons, their symptoms, and the time to onset. Carbon monoxide doesn't fit. Nor does cyanide. She starts looking into cholinergics, checking the many pesticides, when the passenger door opens and a statuesque blonde strides in.

"Dr. Steele?"

"Yes."

"I'm Amanda, the cruise director. I came to speak to you about my father. He and my mother were your patients. Room 636."

"Oh."

Emma studies her with interest. So this is the woman who supposedly tried to kill her parents. She doesn't look like a killer. With her floral yoga pants stretched on perfect legs, baby blue eyes, and a blonde ponytail, she looks like the girl next door going for a quick run.

But she's not. Her sharp cheekbones and the deep lines on her neck tell Emma that this lady is no longer a girl. She's beautiful, sophisticated, and classy but no longer young.

"How is he doing?"

"Your mother is very well."

"And Father?"

"He's OK. But why don't you ask him? I can't tell you much without his permission."

"I understand. But he's got severe dementia and seldom remembers who I am. He only ever recognizes Mother. But I have his power of attorney. I make decisions on his behalf."

"May I see it?"

The papers are in perfect order, dated two years ago. But Emma didn't forget Marico's wild remarks nor the captain's warning to keep her mouth shut. Not to mention that she really doesn't know what happened. All she has are suspicions.

"I think your father and mother got exposed to something which made them sick. I don't know what that was, but..."

Amanda shakes her head.

"I bet it's his medications. And this isn't the first time, you know. Mother is supposed to give them to him, but sometimes she forgets. Or gives them to him more than once. A few times, she took them herself. I always make a point of stopping by to prepare them for her, but last night I had an emergency. The illusionist got so drunk that he couldn't perform the evening show, so I had to come up with a replacement. I didn't make it to their cabin, but I called Mother to remind her. She's better than him, but she also has a touch of dementia. And she has her bad moments, especially in the evening."

"So you didn't get to see them yesterday?"

"No."

Marico said she smelled her perfume. Emma smells it now, even from six feet away. It's a sweet, heavy scent that's hard to miss. She didn't smell it last night, but she had plenty on her plate between the sick patients and her claus-trophobia. No wonder she missed it.

Emma clears her voice.

"It must be hard for your mother to look after your father, especially if she also has dementia."

Amanda shrugs.

"She doesn't really look after him; she mostly keeps him company. I help her bathe him every morning, then I take him for a walk. They can order room service whenever they don't feel like walking to the restaurant. The stewards look after the room, their laundry, and everything else. It's not a bad life."

Emma remembers the room — a disaster, so cluttered she had to fight the urge to run. Whoever looks after it is doing a lousy job. But there's no point in going there.

"It sounds like a good life for your father, but it must be hard for you to look after them besides doing your job."

"There was no other way. They can no longer manage by themselves, and I didn't have the heart to put them in a nursing home and leave them there. I'm away for months, and they have no one else. And I'm lucky. My hours are flex-ible. Unless I have a crisis, I can always steal an hour or two to check on them."

"What do you do on the ship?"

"I make sure the passengers have a wonderful time every hour of every day. If they get bored, we're in trouble. That's why you have to keep them busy. I plan events, classes, and contests and schedule the entertainment and the lectures. And whenever something falls apart, I jump in to replace it.

"That's where it gets iffy. Like when we're supposed to go ashore, but the weather goes bad. Or a shore excursion gets canceled. I need to come up with something to keep them busy and happy, whether it's organizing an eating contest, a trivia game, a dance tournament, or putting up a show on a half-hour notice.

"What do your parents do when that happens?"

"The stewards check on them. Or one of my friends."

"Well, that sure sounds better than a nursing home."

"Thank you. I hope so. Will Father be OK?"

"I think so. I kept him here overnight to observe him, but he's much better. Unless something changes, I'll let him go to his cabin tonight."

"Can I see him?"

"Of course."

Amanda's smile takes ten years off her age, making her look warm, kind, and approachable. *This can't be somebody looking to kill her parents*, Emma thinks. Marico must be wrong.

"Thank you for caring for my parents and listening to me. How about lunch one of these days?"

"I'd love to."

Amanda goes to see her father, and Emma returns to her research. She's so engrossed in studying the many ways that pesticides can kill people, from ingestion to inhalation and even transdermally, through the skin, that she doesn't hear Sue until the door slams behind her.

Sue is delighted. Her green eyes sparkle, and her thin red mouth smiles like a cat who spotted a mouse on crutches.

"If I remember correctly, I informed you that this computer is not for personal use. It belongs to Medical and is only here for patient care."

"You did."

"I see. I guess that was not enough. It saddens me no end, but I'll have to write this up and report it to the first officer."

"Please do. But don't stop there. Please make sure to inform the captain too. I'm researching pesticide poisoning, and the captain will be pleased to hear you chose to spread the news. Don't forget to mention that, unlike you, I wasn't browsing Facebook. If you don't do it, I will."

Sue's cheeks turn bright red like she got slapped. She glances at the screen, then slams the door.

Emma sighs. She should know better than to poke the bear, but she couldn't resist. Turning the other cheek is so not her thing.

CHAPTER 16

A long line of patients stretches out the door to Medical as soon as the afternoon clinic starts. The first few grab chairs; the others lean against the white wall, chatting as they wait for their turn. *They look nothing like my usual ER patients*, Emma thinks as she brings them to her office one by one. They're all well-dressed and smiling, and they act like they're at a social function. They greet her politely in a dozen different languages since they come from all over the world: Australians, Brits, Germans, and Americans, with a smattering of Swiss, Japanese, and Portuguese.

Fortunately, they're not sick — they're only here to replace the medications they forgot to bring.

That should be easy, but it's not. Most don't remember the name of the little white pill they take for their blood pressure or cholesterol or how much of it they take. And if they do, it's usually some name Emma has never heard of, since even the same drugs have different names in different markets. That can get iffy, but she does her best with what she has, counting the pills she knows and writing down the rest to research them later. I'll do it on Sue's Facebook computer, she tells herself, and the thought makes her smile.

The work is interesting, and the people even more so. She checks in a tall, silver-haired man who reminds her of Zagarian, and her heart tightens. She hasn't seen him in months. It looked like something might grow between them for a while, but then she left home to sail the world.

He tried to come to see her, but she blew him off since she was too afraid of commitment. She's regretted it ever since, but it's too late. Still, seeing this man that reminds her of him tugs at her heart.

"Welcome, Mr…"

"Doctor. Doctor Freeman."

"Oh, you're a doctor? What specialty?"

His blue eyes crinkle as he laughs.

"Oh, I'm not your kind of doctor. I have a Ph.D. in biology. I lecture on the ship. This evening's lecture is on poisonous Australia."

"Poisonous Australia?"

"Yes. Did you know that Australia is the most poisonous country in the world? It has more venomous snakes, spiders, toxic plants, and just about every other killer you can think about than any other place on earth. Except for humans, of course. When it gets to our kind, there's fierce competition for who boasts the most ferocious killers, and Australia isn't even in the running.

"Australia is a country of extremes, from the luxuriant plant and animal life along its shores to the immense parched desert in its center. And it's far enough from every other place on earth to have created lifeforms that don't exist anywhere else, like the kangaroos and the dingoes. God only knows how many kinds of spiders, snakes, and poisonous plants it has. That's my particular area of interest, you know? If you ever need to know something about poisons and venoms, I'm your man."

He smiles and leans back in his chair to make himself comfortable. Emma would love to hear more, but she can't since her other patients are waiting.

"That sounds fascinating. Now, please tell me, how can I help you?"

He chuckled.

"I can see you're fascinated. Well, I was going to ask for some heartburn relief, but I may as well be honest. I'm here to check you out and maybe invite you for dinner."

"Check me out?"

"My friend told me that the new ship doctor is a beautiful lady, and she's single."

A hot wave of blood floods Emma's cheeks. She knows she's not beautiful, especially not after spending the night looking after a bunch of sick patients instead of sleeping, and dealing with everything else that has happened since. The meeting with the captain feels like a week ago, but it was only this morning. She's got to look like a scarecrow, with her burning eyes, crumpled scrubs, and messed-up hair. Her hand goes to her hair, then she realizes it and goes so mad her blood boils. Seriously?

She leans back, glaring at him and wishing she could throw him out. But she can't; he's her patient. And she's heard worse. At least he didn't curse at her.

"I'm afraid your friend deceived you."

"Oh, no. She never does."

"She?"

"Hanna. Can we do dinner?"

"Dr. Freeman, I appreciate...

"Frank."

"I appreciate your invitation, but I've had two long days and a long night. And I don't go out with people I don't know."

"We wouldn't go out. That's one of the advantages of being on a ship. We can only dine in."

"Thank you. But not tonight."

"Tomorrow?"

"I don't think so. I still have to get through tonight and don't know what tomorrow will bring."

He shrugs and smiles.

"OK then. I'll be back tomorrow."

He smiles and waves as he leaves, and Emma can't help but smile back. He's so cheeky that he's funny. Then she remembers how she pushed Zagarian away and wonders if the ruin of her marriage will hold her off men forever.

CHAPTER 17

Heavy steps pound the pavement, closer and closer. The man is closing in.

Emma runs for her life, even though her chest is ready to burst. She touches the doorknob just as his fingers close around her throat like iron claws. She tries to scream, but no sound comes out. She needs air. She struggles to pull off the murderous fingers crushing her throat, but she can't, and her strength seeps away as she runs out of air. His ocean-colored eyes gaze into hers, and he laughs as the world turns black.

Emma sits up, soaked in a cold sweat. Her chest heaves, and her scrubs stick to her clammy skin. It's the same old nightmare. You'd think she'd be used to it by now since she's had it for months, ever since she had to do the unthinkable to save her life. That memory haunts her every day and wakes her up every night. That memory made her leave her job, her home, and her family to look for a place where the nightmare wouldn't find her. But there is no such place. Her memories follow her everywhere, even in her sleep. The only thing that keeps them at bay is wine. But here, she can't drink herself into oblivion. She's on call 24/7 and responsible for three thousand lives.

She gazes through the porthole above her bed. The world is dark, but for the moon pouring quicksilver over the sea, and quiet, but for the aircon's low hum.

She lays back in bed, hoping the waves will rock her back to sleep, but the cabin walls start closing around her. She needs to breathe, and here she can't. She throws her windbreaker over her scrubs and cracks open the door to see a shadow passing by.

Darn. The last thing Emma needs is company, so she stands quietly, waiting for the shadow to be gone, but the person knocks at the next door instead.

The door stays closed.

"Fajar." It's just a whisper, soft but intense. "Open. I know you're here."

Emma remembers Hanna's words. Fajar loves them and leaves them, she said. But who is this? And how did they get into the locked Medical?

The door opens, and a man slips out, closing the door behind him.

"Come. Let's go for a walk," the man whispers.

"Why? Let's go to your room."

"I need to walk. Let's go."

He puts his arm around her to lead her to the door, but she shakes him off.

"You have someone in there, don't you? That's why you won't let me in. You have another woman in there."

"Shhh! Be quiet! Let's go."

"No. Who's in there?"

"Let's go and talk, baby. If someone hears us and reports, our ass is grass. We'll both get fired. And we can't afford that, either of us. Let's go somewhere quiet where we can talk. Come on."

He drags her out. She follows reluctantly, and the door closes behind them.

Emma stands at the door, wondering whether to go out and risk bumping into them or go back to bed and fight her claustrophobia, when Fajar's door opens again. A shadow slips out, stops to listen, and then glides out the door, following the others.

Emma stares at the darkness. She's unsure what this is all about, but something unsettling fouls the air. It's like some gruesome evil got unleashed, and terrible things are about to happen. Emma feels the bad omen in her bones, and she shivers.

CHAPTER 18

A few days later, nothing has happened, but the feeling of doom is still there. Once again, Emma tossed and turned for most of the night. As soon as the inky darkness of her porthole paled toward blue, she put on her sneakers, grabbed her phone and pager, and headed out for a walk to clear her head.

The Promenade Deck, a third of a mile of wet deck whipped by the wind overlooking the endless sea, goes all around the ship. It's a good place to be alone with your thoughts, Emma thinks, pulling her windbreaker closer. She starts counterclockwise, walking as fast as the slippery deck will allow. The salty wind smells like the sea everywhere but at the stern. At the back of the ship, the whiffs of coffee and bacon take over. The smell of hot grease adds to the moving deck and the lack of sleep, making Emma's stomach quiver.

She stops at the bow, leans against the rail, and raises her face into the salty wind, wishing she were home. She'd be walking the Adirondacks' trails, breathing in the pine scent of the forest and following Guinness, who's always in the lead, her white tail flying proudly like a flag. Once in a while, Guinness would look back with worried amber eyes and wag her tail to encourage her forward.

"Everything OK? Come on, this is good. You're not working, and we're almost there. What a wonderful day!"

That's the magic of dogs. To them, every day is a beautiful day, whether it's freezing sleet, pouring rain, or scorching heat. Their other magic is their love. Emma would rather look in Guinness's eyes than in the mirror. The mirror tells her the truth, but Guinness's eyes tell her that she's the most wonderful human that has ever graced the earth. And no matter how untrue, we all need to hear that every once in a while.

Emma misses her like she'd miss a limb, and she's only been gone for a month. This life of travel and adventure is not quite what she thought she was signing up for.

First, the job. Carrying a pager 24/7 is about as fun as running with your legs tied together. Emma feels like a dog on a short leash that Sue jerks often. She pages her day and night for no good reason. Paperwork due next week is a good excuse to wake her up from sleep. Every day, she interrupts her lunch with some inane question, then smiles like a lipsticked cobra, happy to see her pissed-off.

Fortunately, the patients are fun. They're interested in her and everything having to do with the ship, and they're patient with Emma's clumsiness in cutting, counting, and distributing pills. Seeing them teaches her how other countries do medical care, and figuring out how to replace their meds with what she's got is a welcome intellectual challenge.

The all-you-can-eat buffet overloaded with everything from caviar to cataifs has done her no favors. She cannot help but overeat every time she goes there since she has to try everything; then she feels guilty. Fortunately, thanks to

Sue, she seldom gets to finish the food on her plate. The crew mess is easier, fish heads and all, but it's lonely. The crew glances at her with curiosity, but they never sit next to her, so she's taken to reading a book over dinner.

The evenings are the worst. Emma lies in her cabin watching the news or an old movie on the vintage channel, wishing she was home with Guinness drinking wine.

She misses Guinness, and she misses her wine. The wine in the passengers' venues is mediocre and ridiculously overpriced. Still, the crew mess has a decent Chilean cabernet sauvignon. She bought a few bottles, but she needs to be careful. First, she can't drink like she used to since she's always on call. And second, she doesn't need the rumor to spread. Emma knows she's an alcoholic, but that's nobody else's business.

She breathes in the salty mist and returns to her walk, but the Promenade Deck is no longer hers. The morning crew has started scraping the rust and layering on thick layers of sharp-smelling paint. The passengers are up too, speed-walking zombies listening to the voices in their AirPods. An old lady shuffles, bending over a cane. Half a dozen smokers foul the air in the small smoker's area, coughing the heavy smoker's morning cough.

Oh well. Emma glues her eyes to the water to avoid eye contact. Funny how being among people makes her feel even lonelier. Her eyes mist as she thinks about Guinness, baby Hope, Margret, and even Taylor, even though that girl sucks the air out of every room she's in. Emma misses them, her work friends, her mountains, and everything else she left behind.

She sighs and glances at the sea. Suddenly, the blue water froths as a dozen playful dolphins appear out of nowhere, chasing each other to race the ship. Their sleek, dark bodies jump out of the water, fall back in with a splash, and jump again. Sparkling water drops surround them like crystal rain. A couple of them fall on Emma's face, and she touches them in wonder. She can't believe she just touched the same water drop as a dolphin.

They keep up with the ship, playing like a bunch of kids on recess, and Emma's heart fills with joy. She bursts into laughter.

"Aren't they wonderful?" the limping lady says, her face filled with light.

"Yes, they are."

They both smile, and Emma recognizes Hanna.

"Good to see you again."

"Good to see you, even though you blew off my friend Frank. Or maybe just because of that. He needs to be cut down to size. How are you doing?"

"Better now," Emma says, watching the dolphins fall behind the ship.

"They bring so much joy. It's like kittens and puppies: You can't watch them without a smile. That's one of the perks of living on a ship. You won't get this in your neck of the woods."

"True."

"But you miss home. And that bitch is making your life miserable."

Emma shrugs.

"How about dinner tonight? We can chat and share memories. You can show me pictures, and I'll treat you to a special wine."

Emma doesn't know what to say. She'd love some company, but...

"Frank?"

Hanna laughs. "Nope. He's a grown man; he can take care of himself."

"OK. Thank you."

"See you tonight."

Maybe this will be a better day, Emma thinks. First the dolphins, then Hanna. Maybe...

Her pager goes off, and her phone starts ringing.

CHAPTER 19

Emma picks up the phone, but it's too late. They hung up already. Her pager goes off. Medical, of course. She could try to call back, but Sue never answers. She wants her to stop whatever she's doing and run back, so Emma decides it's not worth calling. She may as well go back.

She rushes toward medical at the other end of the ship, wondering what it is this time, and hopes it's just Sue, not some disaster needing fixing. Ever since she embarked on this darn ship, she's been flying blind, praying she won't kill anyone.

The door to Medical is open, and Emma bursts in to see a familiar sight. A bloody body lies on the stretcher in the waiting room, Marico's on the phone, and Fajar leans over the patient to get vitals.

"What's up?"

"A trauma. We got a call for an unresponsive female. She was found on the third-floor landing. Nobody saw it happen, and nobody knows how long she was there. She's breathing on her own, but she's not talking, and she's only responsive to pain. I don't know if she's concussed, drunk, or drugged, but she's not talking to me," Fajar said.

"Vitals?"

"Not bad."

"Why don't we move her to the ICU?"

"It's not ready. The stewards are cleaning it after the patient who was there last night."

Emma swears through her teeth and leans over the stretcher. A mane of blonde hair covers the bloody face, and the honey-colored skin glows in the cold electric light. Her pulse is fast but firm, and her lungs sound good. Her neck is already immobilized in a C-collar, as it should be.

With a gentle hand, Emma pushes the curls away to uncover her face and check her pupils. She recognizes the oval face with generous lips. It's Gloria, the singer, and Emma's heart tightens. She wonders what happened to her.

"Let's get an IV and labs, please. And let's move her to the ICU as soon as possible, so we can get her monitored. Did you check her neck?" she asks Fajar.

"I did, but I wouldn't rely on it. She's practically unresponsive. We could try an X-ray, but that's almost useless."

Emma nods. Fajar is right. And clearing the neck is not an emergency now that she's immobilized. She palpates her abdomen, which is soft and benign, bends every joint, and tests every bone. Other than a few bruises, nothing looks out of whack, but since Gloria can't complain of pain, it's hard to rule out a fracture or a dislocation. But for now, that's the best Emma can do.

She sighs, wishing she was in her old ER, with her ultrasound machine, the CT, the MRI, and a surgeon on call. It would be nice to have a surgeon set their hands on the patient, even though they're usually grumpy and treat her like a moron. It doesn't feel good, but as long as they help your patient, so what? Emma's ego can fit in a small Tupperware container on a good day, and this isn't one of those.

What the heck happened to Gloria? Did she take a wrong step and fall down the steps? Was she drunk? Did someone push her?

The door slams, shaking the walls.

"What the hell's going on?" Sue asks. Her grating voice gives Emma goose bumps.

"We have a trauma. It looks like she fell down the stairs," Fajar says.

"Alcohol level 250," Marico says.

Emma shrugs. That's a lot. If you are over 80, you're unfit to drive. That may be why she's not responding and could explain why she fell. But it won't rule out other injuries.

"Let me know when you have the rest of the labs," she tells Marico.

The ICU is finally clean, so they move Gloria in and place her on monitors. Emma knows she should be intubating her to protect her airway since the girl is unresponsive to anything but pain, but she hesitates. Gloria's breathing is fine, and she's moving all her extremities; her alcohol level may explain her obtundation. With a bit of luck, the girl is just intoxicated. She needs to metabolize, and she'll wake up tomorrow.

"Let's keep her here and observe her for now. We'll reassess her tonight."

Sue shakes her head.

"How about taking her back to her cabin and letting her sleep it off? Not like we don't have enough to do here without watching a drunk."

Emma feels three pairs of eyes weighing on her. Keeping Gloria here means that somebody will have to watch her every moment, and they're all exhausted and behind on their sleep. But Emma has no choice. She can't just drop an unconscious woman who may have a head injury and a broken neck in her cabin, hoping she'll live.

"Sorry, no can do. How about I take the first shift so you guys can rest? And who knows? She may be up and running before tonight."

The eyes weighing on her soften, and Emma hopes she's doing the right thing. She's trying to be a team player, damn it, even though she's never been on a team like this.

"We still need to find out what happened to her. Marico, can you call security and have them run through the tapes and see what happened?"

Sue frowns.

"What for?" she asks.

"What if somebody pushed her?"

Sue rolls her eyes, but Emma doesn't care. She doesn't know why, but something on this ship isn't right. She knows there's more trouble looming ahead.

CHAPTER 20

It was already past six when the door closed behind Emma's last patient, an elegant lady whose bunions interfered with her high-heeled shoes. She wanted Emma to do something about the thirty years of damage she did to her feet by wearing tight shoes. Emma recommended wider, flat shoes, but the woman didn't like it. Emma shrugged, gave her some Voltaren gel to help with the pain, and sent her on her way, then rushed to her cabin to get ready for dinner with Hanna.

Taking a shower in this bathroom is definitely an acquired skill, Emma thinks when she drops the slippery soap. The shower stall is too narrow to let her bend, so she steps out to pick up the soap and floods the bathroom floor. She curses softly, then gets herself clean and dry. She has no time to dry her hair, so she towels it and gathers it in a tight bun at the nape of her neck. She sees herself in the mirror and laughs. She looks like a flamenco dancer with her hair slicked to her head and her dark eyes too big for her narrow face. Once it dries, her hair will go wherever it wants, but she won't have to look at it. So there.

Between putting on makeup and squeezing into her cocktail dress, hanging her ID over her cleavage, and grabbing her phone, pager, and lipstick, she's fifteen minutes late by the time she gets to the restaurant, and Hanna is nowhere to be seen.

She stands by the wall watching the steady parade of passengers dressed to the nines flow into the restaurant. It's formal night, so they all wear their best and brightest, whether it's a parrot-green nylon pajama or an inconspicuous little black dress that cost a fortune.

They look like birds, Emma thinks. The women look like giant, exotic birds, with colorful plumage sparkling with beads and costume jewelry. The men in dark suits tottering behind them look like a murder of well-fed crows.

Five more minutes pass, and Emma wonders whether she should ask the maître d' about Hanna. But she doesn't even know her name. What would she say? "I'm here to meet Hanna, the old lady who has lived on the ship since her husband fell off a cliff with his zero-turn lawn mower." Emma imagines his face and starts laughing as a steward in green uniform bows to her.

"Dr. Steele?"

"Yes?"

"Miss Hanna is waiting for you at the Ambrosia restaurant. May I take you there?"

"Ambrosia?"

"Yes. Our finest dining venue."

Unlike this one. I see.

Emma follows him up four floors and toward midship to a quiet, softly-lit place half-hidden by potted plants. And there's Hanna, her eyes sparkling and her makeup perfect, sipping on a glass of red.

"So sorry, I..."

"My fault. I should have explained. I never go to the restaurant on formal nights. It's a circus. On formal nights they serve free wine, so everybody goes there. And they get to play dress-up. All the garish colors, loud people speaking all over each other, and the women giving each other venomous looks! I don't need that. This is much nicer."

"It surely is."

Dark, cozy, and understated, Ambrosia looks like a classy New York steak house. It has glowing mahogany floors, dark green walls, and deep leather armchairs that hug you, and Emma loves it. The soft jazz music makes her smile, and the scent of grilled meat makes her drool. She swallows, remembering she had no lunch today. Between clinic, then watching Gloria, and dealing with Sue's hissy fits, she's been going full speed since this morning. Remembering the dolphins makes her smile. Hanna smiles too.

"You just remembered the dolphins."

"How do you know?"

"The wondrous expression on your face. That's why I always walk at dawn. Fewer people, and there's always a chance to see something wonderful."

"Does that happen often?"

"No. If it did, it might become ordinary. Maybe. But there's always a chance."

An important-looking waiter brings the menus. They're leather-bound and too big to fit on the table.

"May I offer you something to start with? Our martinis..."

"She'll have some of the same wine I'm having, please."

"Of course."

He takes a road trip to bring Hanna's wine bottle and presents it to Emma.

"This an excellent Feudi di Guagnano Le Camarde. It's a

blend of Negroamaro and Primitivo grapes from Salento. The vines, aged 45 to 50 years old, are hand-harvested, and the wine is aged in French oak, giving it rich aromas of blackberry, chocolate, and juniper."

He pours just enough to stain the bottom of the glass and steps back, waiting for her reaction.

What will he do if I spit it back in the glass? Emma wonders.

Hanna smiles mischievously like she's read her thoughts and dismisses the waiter.

"Thank you, Emile. We're good."

She lifts her glass to Emma.

"Cheers. I hope you like it. No matter what that pompous ass said, this is a good wine that deserves a fresh palate."

"Cheers."

Emma sniffs the wine.

The man was right; the wine smells like blackberries and chocolate. She twirls it, takes a second nose, and sips. Her taste buds sing. She hasn't had wine so good since... since the last time she saved Taylor's ass, and she thanked her with an exceptional bottle.

"Wow."

Hanna relaxes in her chair.

"Good. You look like a girl who appreciates good wine. I do too. Also, good company. How was your day?"

"It's over."

"That good, eh? You're still on call, though?"

"Always."

"Then let's order some food in case you get called. It would be a pity to miss a nice dinner. I'll have the lobster bisque and the filet mignon au poivre," Hanna tells the waiter, who has returned to pour three more drops of wine.

"Also, the shoestring potatoes with truffle aioli and the creamed spinach."

"Certainly. And you, miss?"

"I'll have the steak tartare and the cioppino, please."

The second glass of wine goes down as smoothly as the first. They settle to chat in easy companionship, and Emma feels her shoulders relax. She sighs and leans back.

"What do you miss most from home?" she asks Hana.

"I miss my son. Sometimes. He's extraordinarily gifted and full of charm, but he's not someone I can take in large doses. He's like shrimp paste: Lots of flavor, but there's only so much you can take before you catch fire. You?"

"Lots of things. I miss being home, and I miss baby Hope, my granddaughter. I wish I could see her grow into a little person every day. I miss the mountains. And even my ex."

"But what's the one thing you miss the most?"

"Guinness, my dog. It sounds foolish, but she's the one I miss the most. She's my best friend, my conscience, and my biggest fan rolled into one. Without her, I feel incomplete. It's like I lost my shadow."

"What kind of dog is she?"

"A German shepherd."

"Well trained?"

"She used to be a military dog, then a protection dog. I got her when she was four."

"Why don't you bring her over?"

"Bring her over?"

"Yes. They allow service dogs on the ship."

"But... I can't have a service dog."

"You may not. But I can."

CHAPTER 21

Emma stares at Hanna, wondering if she heard her right.

"You can?"

"Of course. I'm mobility impaired, remember? I have a large accessible cabin, and I know everyone on the ship, even the captain. And I love dogs. My border collie Ruby died soon after my husband, so I felt very lonely for a while, but I couldn't get another dog since I didn't know what I was doing with myself. It's been years, but I still miss her. I'd love to have Guinness around."

"That's extremely generous of you."

"Not at all. It's actually rather selfish. I would get not only a dog, but your company too. Cheers."

"Thank you, Hanna. Let me think about it."

The first course arrives, and it's more than a course. It's a show. The waiter rolls in a serving table with the ingredients for the tartare artfully arranged: A glistening raw ground beef patty in the middle, surrounded by a thimbleful of pink Himalayan salt, another of ground Jamaican pepper, a bright orange egg yolk in a crystal glass, minute translucent pickles, mustard, and green parsley. And Worcestershire sauce, of course. He chops the pickles and the parsley, then mixes everything together with two forks and the intense focus of a high priest organizing a sacrifice ceremony. Every eye in the restaurant is glued to her plate, and Emma blushes, wishing she could put an end to the fuss.

Finally, the waiter sets the plate in front of Emma with the triumphant air of someone who just scaled Everest, then leaves like a victor.

Hanna laughs.

"That's why I never order the tartare or the Caesar salad. But that's what they do, and I bet you that next time they come here, half of the people watching will order the tartare just to be the center of attention, even if they've never eaten raw meat. How is it?"

Emma spreads the tartare over the crusty French bread and tastes it.

"Delicious. Yours?"

"It's good, even though it's got more calories than I care for. I'll have to skip breakfast."

A shadow covers the table. They look up.

"Hello, lovely ladies. How nice to find you here."

Frank, resplendent in a dark suit and blue tie, towers over them. His eyes are shaded, but his smile is bright.

Emma glances at Hanna, who shakes her head.

"No, I didn't. Hi Frank, how lovely to see you. How are you?"

"Much better now that I see you two. Do you mind if I join you?"

"We're almost done."

"How about if I just buy you a drink then?"

Without waiting for an answer, he signals the waiter,

who brings another chair. Emma and Hanna pull closer to make room.

"What are you ladies drinking? Can we have another bottle?"

The waiter runs to oblige. Hanna's eyebrows go up.

"Oh well. At least we'll get some wine out of you. But that's not how you invite a lady to dinner."

"I tried the other way. It didn't work. Ask her."

"You told me that you came to check me out. How would you feel if somebody told you that?" Emma says.

"Very flattered. Feel free to come to check me out any day, Doctor. You too, Hanna. I can't wait."

Emma can't help but laugh. He's not only handsome, but he's also funny. Even though this macho thing makes her want to hit him over the head with a two-by-four.

He examines the bottle the waiter presents him and nods.

"You ladies have good taste, though I might have to skip a couple meals to pay for this."

"You can eat at the Sea View. That's free."

"I can't. A man of my condition can only lower himself so much. More importantly, I can't eat there because of all my adoring fans who surround me to watch me chew."

"Really!"

"No, not really. But after I give a lecture or two, people recognize me and stop by to talk and ask questions, regardless of whether I'm eating, working out, or snoozing by the pool, half-naked. It's hard to be famous. The paparazzi, you know."

He tastes the wine.

"Just right. What are you guys doing tomorrow?"

"Nothing. Tomorrow it's Darwin. Too hot for me to go out. I'll lay in the cabin and read," Hanna says.

"How about you, Doctor?"

"I don't know yet, Doctor. Depending on the patients, I hope to go out for a couple of hours, but I still have my clinics. And I share my shore time with the second nurse on call because one of us needs to be on the ship at all times."

"Have you ever been to Darwin?"

"No."

"Why don't I show you around then?"

"As I said, I don't know when, or even if I get to…"

"No problem. I'm flexible. Why don't you call me when you're ready to go?"

"I…"

"Listen, Doctor. If you only have a couple of hours, you really need me. By yourself, you're lucky if you make your way out of the port. You'll waste your day and won't see anything. Let me show you around."

"I…"

As if on cue, her pager goes off just as the steward brings over a steaming cast iron bowl with her cioppino. The seafood stew smells like garlic and thyme. Plump shrimps, dark clams, and translucent scallops mingle in the fragrant red sauce, and Emma's mouth waters. She'd kill to have it, but the pager is calling, and every eye in the restaurant is on her.

"I'm sorry, I have to go. Thank you for a lovely evening, Hanna."

Emma stands to leave. Frank slips her a card.

"Call me tomorrow. And don't worry about the cioppino, I'll take care of it. That's my favorite dish."

On her way out, Emma glances back to see Frank pulling her cioppino in front of him, and she's anything but amused.

CHAPTER 22

It's a bright day in Medical. The ICU has been empty since Gloria went back to her cabin. She was nauseous but otherwise fine, so Emma cleared her neck and removed her collar.

"What happened to you?"

"I don't remember. After my show, I went to the Ocean Bar for drinks with some friends, and I can't remember what happened afterward. Except for waking up here."

"They found you on the third deck, at the bottom of the stairs. Do you remember how you got there? Do you remember falling?"

"No. I just remember drinking upstairs, that's it."

"How much did you drink?"

"I don't know. This guy came and bought us drinks. We chatted and laughed, and I can't remember anything else."

"Who was he?"

"I can't recall."

Emma sent her to her cabin to nurse her hangover. Sue smirked. Emma sighed, but she'd have loved to slap that smirk off her face. The woman was really getting on her nerves. Still, what mattered was that Gloria was fine.

And today, she's going to get off this damned ship, goddammit. She hasn't been off since Sydney. They had a few days at sea after Sydney, then stopped at Whitsunday Islands, but Emma was too busy to make it to the beach. But today, she'll get off come hell or high water. She's already prepared her hat, her summer dress, and her sandals, and she can't wait to get rid of the darn scrubs she's worn day and night for a week.

She shares shore time with Marico, who's on second call. The *Sea Horse* is docked from eight to eight, but Emma has her clinics, so they only have six hours to share between them.

The door opens, and Marico comes in.

"Hello. Nobody here? Good. They're probably out and about already."

"Speaking about that. How do you want to divide our time today? You want to go out in the morning or the afternoon?"

Marico shrugs.

"I don't know. I don't feel like braving the heat, and this damn Darwin is hot enough to melt asphalt. That's how it was the last time I was here. Why don't you take the whole day to yourself?"

"Really? Are you serious?"

Emma feels like a kid who has just been told it's Christmas.

Marico smiles.

"Of course. Go have fun. You've worked hard every day; you need a break. Just make sure you're back in time for your clinic; otherwise, Sue will bite your head off."

As soon as the last patient leaves, Emma runs to her cabin and gets changed. She drops the phone and the pager on the bed, grabs her hat and sunglasses, and turns to the door.

The white card on the desk catches her eye.

Frank. He said he'd show her around. He knows the place. And it would be nice to not be alone, for once.

But he's such a conceited, pushy, macho ice-hole.

But he's funny. And interesting. And last night...

After leaving her cioppino behind, Emma returned to Medical expecting to find Sue with one of her chickenshit things. She hoped she'd avoid smacking her. But, for once, it wasn't Sue. An elderly lady with trouble breathing and a fever turned out to have pneumonia. Maybe. Dana was just as good an X-ray tech as Emma was a pharmacist, so the chest X-ray was so overexposed you could hardly tell if it was a chest or a knee. But clinically, the woman had pneumonia, so Emma treated her with antibiotics and breathing treatments before finally sending her to her cabin hours later.

She was starving when she was finally done, but the restaurants had closed. She went to look for some crackers in the Medical kitchen, but they were all out. So she cursed under her breath, drank two glasses of water, and went to her cabin to sleep.

A glimmer caught her eye: a silver cloche on her desk.

The plate under it held a dark chocolate cake, a piece of Tiramisu, and a glass of Bailey's. And a note scribbled on a napkin.

"Thanks for the cioppino; it was excellent. This is to tell you that Hanna and I are thinking about you and hope you get to bed soon. See you tomorrow. XX."

It wasn't cioppino, but it was a nice thought. And it was darn good.

Emma picked up the phone.

CHAPTER 23

The moment Emma steps out of the *Sea Horse's* overworked AC, the heat hits her like a ton of bricks. By the time she has walked down the gang-plank, her pretty red dress sticks to her sweaty legs. *I've never been that hot outside a sauna, and that didn't involve either clothes or sightseeing*, Emma thinks. *This here is not for the weak.*

She wonders how she'll survive this for six hours. But then she doesn't have to. She can return to the ship when she's had it, and Frank can do whatever he wants.

It turns out that Frank wants to take her hand as they reach the pier.

"Let's go. The car is waiting."

Waay too much togetherness, Emma thinks. She tries to shake him off, but he won't let go and drags her through the crowd of sweaty passengers waiting for a taxi at the cruise terminal's door.

"They'll be there for hours," she mumbles.

Frank shrugs.

"These are those who didn't book a shore excursion.

That's a bad idea here in Darwin. There isn't much to do around the pier, and they'll melt before they can walk downtown. There's our car."

He points to a green Jeep parked in the ragged shade of a palm tree.

"When did you book it?"

"Last night. But I didn't know when you'd call, so I told him to be ready anytime."

Emma doesn't know whether to be amused or annoyed.

"What if I didn't call?"

He opens the door and helps Emma in, then climbs on the other side.

"Then you'd have wasted a wonderful opportunity to see Darwin with the most charming and informative tour guide. Isn't that so, Mo?"

Mo's blinding white smile lights up a carved mahogany face framed by wild gray curls.

"Of course."

"Just so you know, Mo isn't a taxi driver. He's a friend. And, lucky for you, he's an aborigine. The best thing about the Northern Territories is the people, and most of them are Native Australian."

"I'm thrilled to meet you, Mo. Thank you for taking the time to show me around," Emma says.

"My pleasure. What would you like to see?"

"She doesn't know since she's never been here," Frank says.

Emma resists the urge to elbow him, and he smiles like he can hear her thoughts.

"What do you think she should see?"

"How long do we have?"

"I must be back by 3:30."

Mo takes off, avoiding the droves of passengers sweating

in the sun. Oh, boy. *This evening clinic will be a fiesta of sunstrokes, sunburns, and syncopes*, Emma thinks. But she'll deal with it later. For now, she's determined to make the most of her time off the ship.

Mo drives smoothly along the empty black highway lined with palm trees.

"Darwin is the capital of the Northern Territory, also known as Never-Never. This is mythic Australia, as big as Alaska but almost empty. With less than a quarter million people, it's one of the least densely populated places on Earth. Most of the land belongs to the Native Australians, but besides Darwin and Alice Springs, it's mostly desert."

"Is it always so hot?"

"Pretty much. Highs are around ninety in the shade throughout the year, but the humidity changes. May to September is the dry season when we get almost no rain. In 2012 we had no rain for 147 days. Monsoon season, from December to March, rains every day. Did you know that we get more lightning strikes than any other place in Australia?"

His eyes meet Emma's in the mirror. She shakes her head no.

"I don't know much about Australia and even less about the Northern Territories. Why do they call them Never-Never?"

"The name comes from an old poem. It may be way older than that, but Bancroft's poem captured people's imagination and pictured the land's soul.

Out on the wastes of the Never-Never
That's where the dead men lie!
There where the heat waves dance forever
That's where the dead men lie!"

Carried by Mo's deep voice, the words touch her heart.

Her mind's eye sees the scorched wasteland and its dead lying somewhere beyond the modern road with its tidy palms.

"I can see it," Emma says. Mo nods.

"I wish you had a few days. I could take you to Alice Springs to see Uluru. But since you only have a few hours, we'll skip Darwin. It's nothing but a city. We'll go to Kakadu Park, Australia's largest national park. It has everything Australia is famous for: monsoon rainforests, gorges, and mangrove swamps. When it rains, water pours down the escarpment in magnificent waterfalls, like Jim Jim and Twin Falls. It also has an extraordinary wealth of wildlife, including our famous saltwater crocodiles. And I'll show you the rock paintings at the sacred aboriginal sites."

"It sounds amazing."

"It is. It's a long drive but beats walking in that heat."

"I'll keep her entertained," Frank says.

"Good. Tell her about the saltwater crocodiles."

"I will. But first, you tell her about Mindil Beach."

Mo laughs.

"See this lovely beach with golden sand and turquoise blue water? It's the famous Mindil Beach. Thousands of people come here to watch the sunset, browse the night markets, and gorge on the delicious Barramundi fish and chips. It's beautiful, and the water is clean and warm. But nobody ever swims here."

"Why?"

"Because of the box jellyfish," Frank says. "They don't look like much, just a translucent blob of goo smaller than your fist, but they are deadly. Their nematocysts contain a neurotoxin so potent that it can kill a kid in minutes. They've had dozens of fatalities. Once inside the body, the venom opens the cellular potassium channels, leading to hyperkalemia and stopping the heart. Even a mild envenomation can lead to such excruciating pain that people get paralyzed and drown."

I hope none of my passengers gets here, Emma thinks. *But with my luck…*

"What can you do about it?"

"You remove the nematocysts with a gloved hand or shave them off with a knife, then pour vinegar over the affected skin."

"Why vinegar?"

"The acid deactivates the nematocysts and prevents further damage. But really, the smart thing to do is to stay out of that water. Swimming is prohibited throughout the wet season when the waters are full of jellyfish, but you can happen upon them in the dry season too. But there's always someone stupid enough to ignore the warnings. That's why they put vinegar bottles under the warning."

"I see," Emma says, hoping her passengers will be wiser than that.

"Then, there are the saltwater crocodiles. Salties, the Aussies call them. They grow longer than 15 feet and weigh more than 2000 pounds, but they swim better than Michael Phelps at the Olympics. They love to eat, and very few are vegetarians."

CHAPTER 24

Mo wasn't exaggerating when he said that Top End, as the locals call Kakadu Park, was not only a national park but a national treasure.

They clambered through red sandstone canyons, past the blue billabongs that mirrored the cloudless sky, to the Jim Jim Falls, twin falls that broke into spumes as the wall of water crushed against the rock 500 feet below. They climbed up the escarpment towering above the wetlands, watching the lazy river coil like a silver snake, and stopped by the green marshes where fake logs snapped into life, splashing the water with their heavy tails to hunt some unlucky prey.

They scampered up steep cliffs to the twenty-thousand-year-old ochre drawings that depicted long-dead ancestors and extinct thylacines that stared them down from the rock wall.

"Is that a cricket?" Emma asked, studying the drawing of a skeletal creature with crooked antennae.

Mo laughed.

"Pretty close. That's Namarrkon, the lightning man. He's the one who splits the sky with his ax to release the thunder and the rain. His children, the red grasshoppers, announce his arrival when the rains start. And that one there is the Rainbow Serpent. He's the creator who carved out the earth as it is and made it a home for all its creatures."

Long-limbed waterbirds with curious eyes stepped from one lotus leaf to another like children playing hopscotch.

"That's the Alligator River. Funny enough, it has no alligators, but it crawls with crocodiles," Frank said.

"What's the difference?" Emma asked.

"Crocodiles are bigger and more aggressive. And, unlike alligators, they can live in brackish water. They have a set of lingual salt glands that allow them to spit out the salt but keep the fresh water. And they have pointed noses," Frank said.

They watched the Jabiru storks squeak, their black necks stretched like arrows in flight, and the magpie geese fly over the emerald pools honking like cars stuck in traffic.

"What are those?" Emma asked, pointing at a row of giant sandcastles.

"Those are termite mounds. They're made of mud and termite saliva, and they can last up to sixty years," Frank said.

"I didn't even know termites had saliva," Emma said.

Frank laughed.

"What do you know about termites?"

Emma shrugged. "That they're pests and eat wooden houses?"

"That too. But termites eat the inside of the dead trees and thus create shelters that other animals live in. They're incredible builders, and they're essential for the ecosystem."

The trip back to Darwin was quiet. Emma was exhausted but sad to leave.

"Did you enjoy it?" Mo asked.

"Very much. I'm sorry to go back."

"Me too. I'm more alive in the park. My ancestors' paintings and nature's force give me strength."

"How often do you get there?"

"Just about every weekend. I go there to feel recharged."

"What do you do, Mo?"

"I'm a youth counselor and a part-time tour guide."

"You have two interesting jobs."

"I do. How much do you know about the Aborigines?"

"Very little. Just that they were here first, and, like native peoples everywhere, they were marginalized."

"True. Our land was stolen, our culture was dismissed, and our lifestyle became untenable. But that's not the worst part. The worst was that they stole our children. Thousands of native children, especially those with mixed blood, were ripped from their mothers and deprived of their language and culture. They were taught to be ashamed of their native blood."

"Didn't your prime minister apologize not long ago?" Frank asked.

"No apologies can return our children their stolen heritage. They aren't white but don't know how to be native. There's a whole stolen generation that's still in limbo. That's why we have a hard toll of disease and addiction, and our life expectancy is twenty years shorter."

"That makes your work even more important," Emma said.

Mo nodded.

"My work is my life. I do my best to help my people and educate visitors about our culture and way of life. I look forward to the day discrimination will stop, and our culture will get the appreciation it deserves."

They reached the ship just in time for the afternoon

clinic. Emma thanked Mo, waved to Frank, and ran up the gangplank to get changed. She was five minutes late, but the waiting room was empty but for Dana sitting at the desk.

"Where's everybody?" Emma asked.

"Up and about, enjoying Darwin. Unless they melted from the heat. You had a good day?"

"I had a wonderful day. But how come you're here? Where's Marico?"

"She wasn't feeling so good, so she asked me to take her clinic."

"What's wrong with her? Should I go see her?"

Dana shrugged. "Something she ate, maybe? Don't worry; she'll yell if she needs anything. And speaking about that, security wants to speak to you."

"Why?"

"They didn't say."

"Ok. Maybe about my ID? I'll go see what they want."

Emma wandered through the long empty hallways looking for security. The ship was quiet since the passengers and much of the crew had gone ashore. *It's good to have a breather*, Emma thought, opening the door to security.

The officer sitting at the desk put down the phone he was playing on and measured her with a furrowed brow.

"I'm Dr. Steele. I understand you called me."

"Yes. Was it you who had us check the security tapes for that fall?"

"Yes."

"Why?"

"I didn't know what happened to the patient and wanted to ensure there was no foul play."

"What made you think about foul play?"

"I don't know. Just a hunch?"

"You get these hunches often?"

Emma stared him down. The man was unfriendly, bordering on rude. And it was none of his business what in Emma's past made her suspicious. His business was to do his job.

"You realize how busy we are?"

"No, I don't."

He didn't look busy. He sat in his cozy office playing games on his phone. But Emma didn't think mentioning it would help.

"We are busy. We are responsible for everything on the ship and everybody that comes in or leaves. We have no time to go on a wild goose chase because of some hunch."

Emma's blood rushed to her face.

"So you're mad at me because I had you check the tapes, and you didn't find anything. Well…"

"No. I need to know why you had us check those tapes. Because I don't believe in hunches, and somebody pushed that girl down those steps."

CHAPTER 25

My Dear Emma,

I'm glad to hear that you are doing well and enjoy your work on your ship. Your new boss Sue sounds like a lovely person. I'm happy you get along so well, but I'm not surprised. Who wouldn't love you?

All is well here in Upstate NY, even though the weather has been getting to me. A couple of days ago, we had our first snow — just a dusting, but it reminded me that winter is coming. I wish you could send us some of your beautiful sunshine and the blue seas.

Taylor is doing well. She keeps herself busy, as always. She's been in a good mood lately, mainly thanks to her many new freshmen friends. She's very popular, and so is Hope, whom she often takes to class with her. She hasn't figured out what she wants to do, so she changes her mind daily. The last three have been art, premed, and religion. We'll see what she switches to next week.

Little Hope is no longer so little. She's learned to turn from her front to her back, and she was very proud of her achievement until she got stuck and started screaming like a banshee. Fortunately, Guinness learned to nose her back to her stomach, and now they've made it into a game.

I don't know who she looks like because she changes every day. Still, I can already tell she's got your ruthless determination and cheeky sense of humor.

Victor and Amber'second honeymoon seems to be over. Amber got tired of trampling through the November mud in the Adirondacks, and she's back to her nail salons and hairdressers. Victor takes Guinness and the girls up the mountains whenever he's not on call.

The girls are all OK, the human and the canine. They all send you their love and are working on their presents lists from you. I didn't read it all, but the first item is a kangaroo. I hope your bag is big enough.

Guinness is well, but she misses you terribly. Even when she plays with Hope or takes me for a walk, she will get that faraway look that tells me she's there, with you, rather than here. Do you hear her calling? But don't worry about her; we all love her and do our best to keep her busy.

Your friend, the policeman, stopped by the other day. At first, I got startled and wondered if Taylor got in trouble again. But it turns out he only came to ask about you. He hopes you are well and sends his regards. Don't hesitate to drop him a note, he said. His email address hasn't changed.

I'm OK. Sadly, gardening is over this year, but I have Vera's books to study through the winter and plan for spring.

This will make you laugh: I've been enjoying the attentions of a gentleman I met online. Taylor convinced me to try online dating — it will help pass the long winter nights, she said. She was right. The gentleman — his name is Charles — is not what you'd expect. He's not into gardening; he's much more into sports. He used to be a marathon runner and a vet. That should come in handy in case a war breaks out, and I need advice. He invited me *for a run on our first date, but at my age, that's not something I'd envision unless chased by some dangerous creature.*

"How about tea instead," I said.

We settled on dinner, and I must admit that his carbonara was almost as good as mine. He's pretty good with wine, too, even though he seems to be more into whites. His Sancerre was as good as any I had. You two will have to compare notes someday.

Dinner was good, but after that, things got a little dicey. He became exceedingly friendly. But I hadn't planned on a sleepover, so I didn't bring my denture cup. That's what I told him, but honestly, it's not about the dentures. It's been a long time since I laid in someone else's bed, and I'm OK with that. Then why go on the dating site, you ask? Well, for the fun of it, primarily. And companionship. But you do have a point.

Either way, I slept in my own bed that night, and I thought the romance was over, but last night he called to invite me for a hike. That should be interesting since I haven't hiked since I had Victor forty-some years ago. I'll let you know how it went if I make it back.

That's all I've got. Stay safe and have fun. We all love you, miss you, and can't wait to hear your news and see your pictures. Give my best regards to Sue and tell her your ex-mother-in-law is grateful she's so kind to you.

Love

Margret and the gang

CHAPTER 26

Emma sets aside Margret's email to look for the wine she hid in the wardrobe. It's there for desperate situations, and it seems that tonight qualifies.

She opens it — fortunately, like most Chilean wines, it has a screw top — and pours a third of it into her mug. Pathetic, indeed, but crystal wine glasses are hard to come by in the crew mess. *Just as hard as good wine*, she thinks, shivering as the sharp wine burns her throat.

She lied to Margret, of course. Between Taylor, Hope, and Guinness, Margret has enough to worry about; she doesn't need to worry about Emma, too, even though she's more of a mother to Emma than her own ever was. Ten years ago, when Victor left Emma and Taylor to marry his new trophy wife, Margret told him what she thought about him and sided with Emma. And even though she eventually made peace with him — he's her only son, after all — she's still Emma's best friend.

Emma misses her. She misses them all, especially Guinness and Hope. She even misses Victor. Amber? Not so much. But her heart aches, knowing it will take months before she sees them again.

Even worse, she's starting to hate the ship. The pager, the phone, the narrow cabin with its dirty porthole that never lets in any sun, the strict hours for her clinics, and the fact that she never has a day off. Not even ten minutes without the darn pager. She was getting used to it, but just a few hours off the ship reminded her what life was like when she was a free person. Coming back to the boat was like coming to jail.

And then, to top it off, finding out that Gloria didn't fall down those stairs on her own. She had help.

She'd stared at the security officer, hoping she'd heard him wrong.

"Somebody pushed her? Who?"

He shook his head.

"Can't tell. It's just a few seconds of film. Let me show you."

He turned to the monitor on his desk and pushed a button. A grainy black-and-white video showed the stairs. The door opened seconds later, and two dark silhouettes came through. They were nothing but shadows, impossible to recognize. The first one took two steps down. The other followed, then shoved the first one, who tumbled down a dozen steps and landed below in an immobile heap. The upper shadow left through the door it came in.

"Can you recognize them?"

"No. I can't even recognize the victim, even though I know her. Why is the image so bad?"

"Hah. The lighting is bad, and those cameras are older than dirt. Do you think the company has money to sink in new security equipment? It's all for show. Fresh flowers, crystal glasses, caviar, and whatever crap to impress the passengers. Safety? Who cares about safety?"

He turned off the monitor.

"Tell me about your hunch. Where did it come from?"

Emma shrugged.

"I'd tell you if I knew, but I don't. I just have a gut feeling something bad is about to happen. And my gut never lies."

"OK, doctor. Please come back to tell me if your gut has any other news. Though I'd rather that it settled."

"Me too."

Back in Medical, Dana checked her with sharp eyes.

"What did he want?"

"He... said he didn't find anything on those tapes I asked him to check."

Dana nodded, and Emma wondered why she had lied to her.

The truth is that she doesn't trust her. She doesn't trust any of the people in Medical. Something terrible lurks here, something dark and threatening. Sue's a bitch, of course, but that's not it. And even after all this time, there's still no explanation for all those sick folks.

And there's more. Someone has been going through her things. When she returned from Darwin this evening, she found that someone had gone through her drawers, and the thought of some stranger touching her underwear gave her the heebie-jeebies.

She suddenly remembers the nurse who killed herself. Nadja. Why doesn't anyone ever mention her? Why did she kill herself? Or did she?

Emma pours herself another mug of wine. She knows she shouldn't, but that's the only way she'll get any sleep.

She thinks about Mo and his passion for his people and their plight. How can this beautiful land be burdened by so much misery? Why do so many have to struggle with such unfairness?

She's lucky to have choices. She hates the ship, but it was her choice to come here. And in a few months, she can go home. Sooner, if she needs to. They won't tie her to the medical desk! But Mo and his people have no place to go. Their only choice is to fight for the justice they deserve.

Frank was right. She'd have wasted the day melting on Darwin's streets if she hadn't called him. She wouldn't have met Mo to learn about the Aborigines. Or about box jelly-fish, termites, and crocodiles. Frank may be an asshole, but he's challenging, stimulating, and fun. Not hard to look at either.

She drains her mug and checks what's left in the bottle. Not much. She'd finish it if she were home. But not here. Somebody may need her soon, and she needs to be ready.

She corks the bottle, puts it away, and turns off the light.

CHAPTER 27

The red rock is hot and tall enough to hold the sky. Twin waterfalls crumble from the top of the cliff to the ladder that starts at Emma's feet. Up above, a rainbow snake stares at her, his bifurcating tongue whispering something Emma can't understand. She sets her foot on the ladder's first rung when an immense red cricket splits the sky with his axe. The thunder strikes the snake, and he falls, his silver scales ringing like bells as he tumbles down toward Emma. He falls on her and coils around her throat, tighter and tighter. He smiles, and his familiar ocean-blue eyes gaze into Emma's. The bells get louder and louder, and Emma sits up in her bed, drenched in sweat.

She gasps, trying to remember where she is. In her cabin, of course, and her phones are both ringing.

"Hello."

"Bright Star."

"Coming."

She grabs her black bag and blasts through the door before realizing she forgot to ask where. A Bright Star can be anywhere on the ship, and she doesn't know where to go. Fortunately, Dana's just running out with the Bright Star code bag, so Emma follows her up the steep metal steps.

"Where?"

"703."

They take the steps two at a time, and Emma's out of breath by the time she opens the door to the seventh deck. Cabin 703 turns out to be hidden. It's off a narrow hallway behind locked metal doors at the very bow of the ship. Dana unlocks the door with her universal key and steps aside. Emma runs in to find a sweaty Fajar performing CPR on whoever's lying in the bed.

Unlike the other passenger cabins, 703 is small and spartan. It has a desk, a bed, and a loveseat that has seen better days. There's something strangely familiar about it, but Emma doesn't have time to think about that. She steps to the head of the bed to see the livid face half-covered by blonde hair and realizes what's familiar. It's the scent. The code is for Amanda, the cruise director, and Emma's heart skips a beat.

"Let's move her to the floor."

Emma grabs her arms and Fajar her legs to lay her on the floor, where the hard surface allows for better CPR than the mattress. The stretcher crew arrives, and a man kneels by the body, taking over the CPR. Fajar steps back, his chest heaving with effort.

Emma kneels to check the neck for a pulse. No pulse. She pulls up an eyelid to expose wide, dilated pupils that don't react to light. The woman is dead.

Never mind. They have to give her every chance, so she places the oxygen mask on her face and squeezes the blue bag to push air into her lungs.

"Let's get an IV and give Epi."

Dana kneels to get IV access. The rest of the team waits for their turn to do CPR.

Emma turns to Fajar.

"What happened?"

"I... I came to see Amanda. She was unresponsive. I checked for a pulse and couldn't find it. So I called the Bright Star and started CPR."

Emma glances at her watch. It's almost midnight.

"Why did you come to see her?"

Fajar looks down.

"She... she and I, we...."

"You had an affair?"

"Yes."

"Does she have any medical problems that you know of?"

"Just diabetes."

"Insulin-dependent?"

"Yes."

"Got the IV," Dana says.

"Let's check the glucose and give her an amp of D50. Epi first."

His face dripping with sweat, the man doing CPR moves aside to make room for another. Dana pushes in the Epi as Sue blasts in through the door.

"What's going on?"

She stares at Fajar and Emma, then at Amanda, still and unconscious, and gasps.

"Glucose is 12."

"Did we give the D50?"

"Yes."

"Give another, please. Sue, can you get a second IV?"

Sue's lips tighten in a line, but she kneels to work on the IV.

Emma checks her watch.

"Let's give another Epi, please. And another D50."

Minutes pass like years. Exhausted, the man doing CPR steps aside to make room for the next. Sue secures a second IV, and they run fluids, but nothing helps. Amanda's face has turned blue, and Emma wonders how long she'd been dead before Fajar found her.

They do their best, but nothing makes a difference. Amanda is dead, and she stays that way.

Emma calls the code.

"It's twenty-three minutes past midnight. Thank you all for your good work. You couldn't have done more."

The men lift the body back to the bed and file out of the room. Fajar, his eyes wet with tears, brushes the hair away from the pale face and kisses her cheek.

Dana straightens the covers over the body, then collects the medical debris scattered over the floor. Sue picks up the phone.

"Captain? We have a body. No, nothing else we can do. We'll clean up the cabin and bring her folks to visit before we move her. Yes, I'll deal with that."

"Where do we move her?" Emma asks.

"To the refrigerator."

CHAPTER 28

Telling a parent that their child was dead had always been Emma's most dreaded part of the job. Even worse than telling someone they have cancer. She hates that too, but it comes with the job.

She returns to her cabin to splash cold water over her face, brush her teeth, and put on her white coat, then goes to cabin 636.

She knocks and knocks, then rings the doorbell, but no one answers. She sighs and opens the door with her passkey, hoping they won't have a heart attack.

She turns on the light.

They sit up and stare, the mother with her short wisps of white hair spiking out, the father with his mouth half open, drooling on the left side. They hold hands.

"I'm afraid I have bad news for you," Emma says, moving a pile of clothes off a chair to sit.

They stare at her in silence.

"Your daughter, Amanda, has died."

"Who?" the man asks.

"Amanda. Your daughter."

"What happened to her?"

"She died."

"Who died?"

"Your daughter Amanda died."

His mouth open, he stares at her without understanding.

The woman's watery blue eyes fill with tears. She sobs. Then, as if a dam broke, she screams and cries again. She covers her face with her hands. The harsh sobs shaking her fragile frame make her sound like a wounded animal.

Her husband turns to her, his eyes wide. He pats her shoulder, touches her tears, then stares at his wet finger.

"Why are you crying?"

Emma wishes she was anywhere else but here. What will they do? With Amanda gone, they won't be able to live on the ship, even if they can afford it. Will they go to a nursing home? Who will make the arrangements? And who will make arrangements for Amanda?

Emma listens to the mother's sobs, and the terrible grief breaks her heart. She wants to cry, but she can't. So she waits quietly until the woman uncovers her face.

"What happened to her?"

"We're not sure. She was found dead in her cabin."

"Shot? Stabbed?"

"No. Just dead."

What a strange question, Emma thinks.

"Would you like to see her?"

"Yes."

The woman gets out of bed in her old-fashioned white nightgown with tiny ruffles and heads to the door.

"How about a robe?"

Emma grabs the white terry robe hanging on the bathroom door, helps her put it on, and heads to the door.

"What should we do about your husband?"

The woman lays him back in bed, covers him to his chin, and kisses his forehead.

"You go to sleep, dear. I'll be back."

She turns to Emma.

"Let's go."

Amanda's cabin is clean and tidy. White and beautiful like a porcelain doll, Amanda lies in her bed, her eyes closed like she's sleeping. The security officer standing by the door moves aside to let them in.

The woman sobs and sits on the bed to hold her daughter. She caresses the white face and touches her hair crying softly.

"So it was true. I hoped it was a mistake. I hoped it was somebody else's daughter. But it really was you. What happened to you, Amanda? Where did you go? Why did you leave us? You promised to care for us and close our eyes when we died. And now?"

She rocks gently, holding her daughter's hand. She presses it to her lips and touches the gold band on her finger.

"What will happen to us? And what will happen to your fiancé? He'll be heartbroken."

"Her fiancé?" Emma asks.

"Yes. Did anyone tell him?"

"Not that I know of. Is he on this ship?"

"Of course. That's how the two of them met. He's such a nice young man, and he loves Amanda very much."

She touches the pale dead face and sobs.

"He loved her very much. They were going to get married next fall. She had already picked her wedding gown. I asked her: "Amanda, aren't you too old for a wedding gown?" She didn't care. She said she wanted a white wedding, the flowers, the little girls carrying her train

— all of it. And she was entitled. Why not? She'd never been married before. She had even booked a nice venue. 'We'll have a rustic wedding,' she said. She booked this old barn in an apple orchard. She dreamed about their pictures embracing amongst the apple trees heavy with fruit against the old red barn."

She wipes her eyes with her sleeve. "Poor boy. He'll be heartbroken."

"Who is he?" Emma asks.

"And what am I going to do about your father? I can't care for him by myself. I'll have to put him in a nursing home. He won't know anybody there, and he'll be so scared and lonely. Who will put him to bed at night? Who will take him for walks? Who will give him his meds? And cut his meat? You know how he needs it cut really small because of the dentures. Oh, Amanda, what am I going to do?"

She breaks into sobs again, holding her daughter. Her forehead resting on Amanda's chest, she cries and cries.

Emma sits on the ratty old sofa and wipes her eyes with the back of her hand.

It feels like forever until the woman sits up and glances out the window at the ship's bow, lit like a Christmas tree against the dark sky and the shimmering sea.

"I hate the sea. I told Amanda when she took this job that she shouldn't. It wasn't a good place for her. But she didn't listen. She never did. She said that this way, we can all be close, and she'll take care of us, and we'll have a good time. Then she met her fiancé, and it looked like she was right. The sea was good to her. And now..."

Her voice is raw from crying. Emma opens the little fridge under the desk and hands her a water bottle. The woman empties it and sets it on the desk.

"Now what?"

"I'll take you back to your cabin and speak to the captain about arrangements. And talk to Amanda's fiancé, of course. What's his name?"

"Fajar."

CHAPTER 29

The captain looked like he'd slept in his crisp white shirt.

"What happened to her?"

"If I had to guess, I'd say Amanda died due to an insulin overdose."

"Are you sure?"

"No. She needs an autopsy, and that's not in my job description. But she was fine earlier; then she was dead. Her very low blood sugar screams insulin overdose to me."

"How do you overdose on insulin?"

"Easy. You take more than you should."

"Why would she do that?"

"What makes you think she did that?"

"The suicide note."

"Suicide note?"

"Yes. She left a suicide note."

"Where?"

"On her phone."

"May I see it?"

The captain gave her a side look, then handed her a paper.

"You said her phone."

"It's in custody for the police. This is the printout."

Emma read the paper.

"Dear Mom and Dad,

I'm so sorry to leave you like this. I've been trying hard to hold it together for months, but I can't do it anymore. My depression has been getting worse and worse, and it feels like life has no meaning to me. I just can't continue suffering like this. Please don't be upset. I will at least have stopped suffering, and I hope we'll all be together someday. I love you.

Amanda."

Emma shook her head and dropped the paper on his desk.

"Well?"

"This is BS."

"What are you talking about?"

"Amanda didn't kill herself. She was planning an orchard wedding. She had bought a dress. She was caring for her elderly parents. She had no reason to kill herself."

The captain's eyebrows rose. "How do you know all this?"

"I just spoke to her mother. Who, by the way, asked me what happens next. I told her I'd speak to you, and we'll let her know."

"Who was Amanda going to marry?"

"Fajar."

"Fajar? But he's married. He just asked permission for his wife and kids to come on the ship in Semarang."

"Come on the ship?"

"Yes. Semarang is Indonesia. We do our best to allow our Indonesian crew members to spend the day with their families when we're there. Many choose to bring them on the ship to show them where they live and work when they're away from home. We make it into a celebration. We decorate the ship and set up tours, music, and an ice cream bar. But they have to ask permission first. I just signed Fajar's permission two days ago."

The captain opened a drawer and rummaged through the folders.

"There it is. Anissa, wife, and two kids, Ajar, age 8, and Fitry, age 4.

"I wonder if Amanda knew."

"Obviously not."

Emma shrugged. Things are rarely obvious. It would have been hard for Amanda not to know. Everybody, even Emma, knew that Fajar was married. But maybe she thought the marriage was falling apart?

"Maybe he told her he was getting a divorce? Maybe that's why the wedding was planned for the fall, almost a year from now." Emma said.

"But if he brought his wife and kids on the ship, she was bound to find out. Maybe even meet her. She would have known they were still together," the captain said.

"Exactly."

"Maybe that's why she died. She found out that Fajar lied. He wasn't going to leave his wife, and all the plans for her dream wedding were just a pipe dream, so she killed herself," the captain said.

"Maybe. But wouldn't Amanda say it in her suicide note, then? 'I found out that my fiancé lied to me, and I can't live with the pain'?"

The captain sighed.

"Maybe. Or maybe she was too proud and didn't want to give Fajar the satisfaction of knowing she killed herself for him."

"Maybe. Or maybe she didn't kill herself," Emma said.

"Well, she's dead."

"I couldn't help but notice. But maybe somebody else killed her."

The captain's eyes widened.

"Fajar? Are you crazy? He's a good man! And a doctor!"

Emma shrugged.

"If you knew doctors like I do... And I didn't say it was him, but it could have been. He was the one who found her. And he went into her room at midnight. Who else would she let in in the middle of the night? Who had access to her phone to leave the suicide note? Who has access to insulin?"

"You just told me that you didn't know it was the insulin. And Amanda must have had her own insulin, so anyone could have given it to her," the captain said.

"Insulin is an injection. You think she'd stay put waiting for someone to inject her, then stay put for hours waiting to die?"

"I don't know what I think. But I don't like it. Do you always carry a black cloud?"

Emma thinks about her last year and all those who died around her.

"Often."

"Well, Dr. Black Cloud, we'll take the body to the morgue and seal the cabin for police to process. We should have done it long ago before having everybody traipse through it, but it's too late to worry about that."

"What will happen to her parents?"

"Damned if I know. We'll have to contact their relatives

and see who can take charge of them. We'll have to disembark them as soon as possible. They can't stay on the ship."

"Where will you disembark them?

"Our next stop is Komodo. There's nothing there but a bunch of fat dragons and a couple of villages. No place for them to go. But after that, we're in Lombok, in Bali. That's a big port. We'll talk to the company shore representative and have them arrange for their care and transportation."

The captain stood, signaling the end of the meeting.

"I don't think I need to remind you that you should keep your suspicions to yourself," he said. "Are you a psychic in your spare time, by any chance? I heard about your hunch about the singer that fell down the stairs. Now, this. How about taking it easy for the next few days?"

"I'll try to refrain."

The sky faded to pink by the time Emma reached her cabin. She sat on her bed, looking at the glorious sunrise Amanda would never see, and cried.

CHAPTER 30

Two days later, Emma has a new spring in her step. Today, she's going ashore for the first time since Darwin, and she can't wait to get off the darn ship. Frank asked her to join him, but she'd already signed up for the subsidized shore excursion the company organized for the crew. His cocky attitude gets on her nerves, and she can't wait to be among happy, smiling people for a change.

Since Amanda's death, Medical has been as much fun as a funeral home out of business. Fajar makes himself scarce unless he's in clinic. Sue's thin mouth is shut so tight it looks zipped. Marico's eyes are red and swollen like she's been crying. Even Will, who always greets Emma with a smile, seems put off.

The only one who didn't change is Dana, who's on first call today. She hums a song as she empties the autoclave and puts away the sterilized instruments. *Her voice is nothing to write home about, but this place is way overdue for some joy*, Emma thinks. *What a lovely girl!*

"I'm so glad it's you! Everyone else has been acting funny lately. What's wrong with everyone?"

"Sue and Fajar had a big run-in the other night. I was in the ICU with a patient, and they were too worked up to keep their voices low. Sue asked Fajar why he'd gone to see Amanda in the middle of the night. He told her it was none of her damn business and she'd better worry about her husband instead. Now they no longer talk unless they must."

Dana laughs, and a cheeky dimple shows up on her left cheek.

"I can't say I'm sorry to see Fajar at the bottom of the barrel. He was long overdue."

"Anything I can do?"

"Yes. Ignore them. You know, Emma, we live with each other for months, sometimes contract after contract. You just arrived, and there's a lot you don't know. And you don't want to. What you don't know won't hurt you. Just ignore them and do your thing."

Emma isn't sure that what she doesn't know won't hurt her. Quite the opposite; she'd rather know than be in a fog. But Dana is right. These people have lots going on that she isn't privy to, and all her questions got her nowhere.

The other day after clinic, she asked Fajar about Amanda, but Sue showed up, and he scurried away. Then she tried to talk to Marico, but she shrugged and sent her back to Fajar. Oh well.

She'll get back to it later, but for now, she's going to enjoy her day off. This crew shore excursion should be fun.

Emma runs to her cabin to change as soon as the last passenger leaves the clinic, then lines up for the tender with the crew. The pier of the Komodo island can't accommodate a massive cruise ship, so the *Sea Horse* has anchored a mile away from the island, and the visitors get tendered in.

That's all new for Emma. She's seen the lifeboats

clinging to the ship like baby possums to their mother, but she has never traveled in one. Watching the orange boat bounce up and down the spirited waves tightens her stomach, so she turns her eyes to the gathering crew. They've ditched their usual uniforms for joyful shorts and T-shirts in every color of the rainbow. They've also ditched their attitude. They're no longer quiet and deferential; they're boisterous and happy. Every day on the ship, they're cooks, sailors, waiters, or cabin stewards, the uncelebrated workers keeping the boat afloat, the cabins clean, and the passengers comfortable. But today, they play like children, laughing, shouting, and chasing one another.

Someone touches her arm.

"Are you coming on the crew excursion, doctor?"

It's Gloria, and she's back to her former glory. Her blonde afro and coral overalls make her stand out even in this colorful crowd.

"I am."

"Me too. How have you been?"

"OK. How about you?"

"Much better, thank you. I had a headache for a day or two, but it's over. And I haven't drunk since."

"Good for you. Did you remember what happened that night?"

"We drank at the bar, then somebody took me to my cabin."

"Who?"

"I don't know. I asked a couple of the girls who were there, but they couldn't remember either. We were all pretty smashed."

They get to the front of the line. The two sailors watching the tender grab Emma's arms to help her step from the *Sea Horse* to the bucking tender. A wave slaps the lifeboat and throws Emma off balance. She falls into the nearest seat, and Gloria takes the seat next to her. She starts talking, but the engine noise drowns her voice.

It's noisy and smoky as heck, but Emma doesn't care. She's just happy to be off that darn ship. She breathes in the sea air and leans forward to catch a glimpse of the island. Surrounded by dreamy turquoise waters, the white beach shaded by green palms looks like a picture-perfect tropical paradise. But the paradise ends at the beach.

Beyond it, the ground is hard, cracked dirt with sparse brown grasses thirsty for water. The "WELCOME TO THE NATIONAL PARK OF KOMODO" signs warn: "DON'T LEAVE YOUR GROUP. FOLLOW YOUR GUIDE'S DIRECTION AT ALL TIMES. DON'T VENTURE AWAY FROM THE PATH."

A dozen rangers in khaki uniforms wait at the entrance, leaning on their heavy sticks. They're not typical smiling tour guides; they're rangers, and they're on a mission: to protect the visitors from the dragons. And maybe the other way around.

"Anybody here bleeding?" a ranger asks.

Emma and Gloria stare at each other.

"The Komodo dragons have an extraordinary sense of smell. They can sense blood from five miles away, and if they do, they're likely to attack. That's why we don't allow menstruating females on the island."

Wow. What happens to the people who live on the island? Are they all men? Emma wonders. But she doesn't get to ask since the rangers line them into a single file with a ranger ahead and one behind, their sticks ready.

"Let's go. Don't step off the path."

"Aren't we getting a little overdramatic?" Gloria mumbles.

Emma agrees. Those dragons look severely overrated.

Lazing on the parched dirt in the ragged shade of the few dusty trees, the dragons are nothing like the sky-splitting, fire-spitting monsters from *Game of Thrones*. They don't look like dragons at all. They're just a bunch of lazy fat lizards the size of SUVs with long tails as thick as tree trunks. Their narrow, snake-like heads look way too small for their bloated bodies. Their eyes closed, they lie in the sun or waddle on thick legs placed too wide on their body, shaking their heads from side to side like they're fighting a hangover and sticking out their foot-long bifurcated tongues.

"What do they eat?" someone asks.

"Meat. The adults live mostly on Timor deer. But they'll hunt pigs, goats, and even their own young. Humans too. The young are great climbers, so they'll eat anything from insects to birds. The adults can kill a buffalo, swallow a whole goat, or unearth bodies. That's why the villagers bury their dead in clay, not sand, and cover them with heavy rocks."

"How on earth can these things catch a deer?"

"They stalk them. But don't be fooled — they can run as fast as twelve miles an hour and swim like you wouldn't believe. If they're too heavy to climb, they'll stand on their back legs and tails to pull the prey down and shred its throat with their inch-long teeth. But even a small wound can be lethal. Their teeth have a poison that stops blood from clotting, so their prey bleeds to death. Their tongue can smell carrion from miles away."

Emma stares at the small porcine eyes. It's hard to believe these ugly creatures are something to worry about. She steps off the path to take a picture of a half-asleep monster lazing in the sun.

She kneels to get a better close-up of the flickering yellow tongue when the monster flips up and falls over his neighbor. Startled, the neighbor opens his gigantic mouth full of yellow teeth and bites the other's throat. With a harsh metallic sound, the sharp fangs slide over the scaly skin like it's armor. The first one hisses and bites back, but he can't break the skin. Seconds later, they're back into their torpor.

The rangers laugh as Emma retreats to safety. She laughs too, but the sudden attack leaves her shaken. With their ugly faces and graceless bloated bodies, these creatures are the essence of evil. Ugly, stupid, and deadly.

CHAPTER 31

Back in her cabin, Emma washes her laundry and hangs it up in the shower like she does every day since she has very little space to dry it. She's almost ready for her clinic when the phone rings.

"Hello?"

"Since you blew me off when I offered to show you the island, how about dinner to show me that you don't hold a grudge?"

"Frank?"

"Yep."

"I'm not sure when I'll be done with the clinic. And even afterward — I never know when I'll get called."

"It's OK. I have time. And I'll sacrifice myself to eat your entrée. Seven?"

"OK. Same place as before?"

"Yes. The Ambrosia is the best restaurant on the ship. It's not free, like all the others, but it's worth it. And I owe you a cioppino!"

Emma finds that she's smiling as she hangs up. There's something about Frank that's half annoying, half endearing, like a puppy chewing on your shoes who licks your face as you scold it. And she can use the company and the conversation, let alone the cioppino!

He's waiting at the door when she arrives at Ambrosia, five minutes early. He looks handsome and sharp with his crisp white shirt and perfect hair, and Emma wishes she wasn't wearing the same black dress she wore the last time. But she didn't have a choice. Her two suitcases had to hold everything from the old doctor's bag with all her trinkets and her books to her winter clothes, so she's a bit short on dress-up options.

"Hi."

"You didn't stand me up!"

Emma laughs.

"To be honest, I was tempted."

"I knew it. Why?"

The maître d' takes her arm to lead them to the table in the corner, where an emaciated pianist dressed in a tuxedo slides his long fingers along the keys playing Gershwin.

"Wine?" Frank asks.

"Of course."

He whispers to the waiter, who nods and disappears, then turns back to Emma.

"So, why did you want to stand me up?"

"It's been a long day, and I..."

"Emma, cut the crap. I don't care about bullshit. Why?"

Emma looks into his intense blue eyes.

"Well, to be honest, you're a little much."

"How so?"

"You won't take no for an answer. You act like you're always right and behave like God's gift to women."

"But I am!"

He stares at her with the utmost conviction, and Emma bursts into laughter.

"I'm also well-informed, funny, and utterly charming. So there."

Emma laughs even louder. The waiter brings the wine and shows him the bottle. Frank nods.

"Let's taste it."

The waiter pours just enough to stain the bottom of the glasses, then disappears with the bottle. Frank shakes his head.

"I hate it when they do that. Then they stalk you and pounce on your glass to pour more whenever you take a sip."

Emma sniffs the wine. Black currant, cedar, and rose. She takes a sip. Substantial but smooth.

"Lovely wine. What is it?"

"A Pauillac. 2015 Grand-Puy-Lacoste. Now, admit it. You were pissed I didn't ask you what wine you wanted."

Emma nods sheepishly.

"I didn't ask because I didn't want to give you something you knew. I wanted to show you something new. Life is more interesting when we try new things. Now tell me why you didn't stand me up?"

"I almost did."

"Why didn't you?"

"For the cioppino."

Frank laughs so hard that the piano player turns to stare. Frank waves and the man smiles and gets back to his keys.

"He's great. He should be playing in a concert hall, not here."

The waiter comes to refresh their drinks and take their order.

"I'll have the Caesar salad and the salmon, please. And please leave the bottle; we're old enough to pour."

The man's mouth narrows, but he sets the bottle on the table and turns to Emma.

"I'll have the cioppino."

"And for an appetizer?"

"She'll have the cioppino as an appetizer," Frank intervenes. He turns to Emma.

"Otherwise, they'll only bring it with my salmon, and you may miss it again. You can have a second one as a main dish."

He's right, of course, but he's so arrogant Emma wants to kick him under the table. She refrains and sips on the wine instead.

"How did you like the dragons?"

"Not much. They're nothing like I imagined them."

"Few things ever are. And they are dirty, evil creatures, even though much of the stuff is exaggerated. They only had a few dozen fatalities due to them altogether, most of them because of wound infection. I wish somebody would teach them to brush their teeth."

"How about the poison?"

"Legend, mostly. They secrete some proteins that interfere with coagulation, but their effect is highly exaggerated. But the more hype they get, the more tourists come, and the more money for the park. Understandable, really, but not necessarily accurate. You should come to my lecture tomorrow night. You'll enjoy it."

"What is it on?"

"Come, and you'll find out."

Emma laughs.

"At least you're consistent. Tell me about yourself."

"Why?"

"Because I want to know how you got to be the way you are. Are you retired?"

"Of course."

"From what?"

"The army. Then I worked with the Smithsonian on their snake collection for a few years."

"Married?"

"Divorced. Three times."

Emma laughs.

"I wonder why. Kids?"

"One daughter."

"Grandkids?"

"Two boys. Two and four. Is the interrogation over?"

"They call it a conversation."

"Who does?"

"People. That's how they get to know each other. You tell them about you and ask them about themselves."

"I see."

He takes another sip of wine, looking into Emma's eyes.

"What's your favorite snake?"

Emma chokes on her wine, then blots the spillage, thankful that her dress is black.

"I'm... not that much into snakes."

"Spiders then?"

"Spiders?"

"Yes. Did you know that the Sydney funnel-web spider is the most venomous in the world? It doesn't look like much and is only an inch long, but it has fangs larger than a brown snake that can pierce toenails. Their venom is neurotoxic. The male's bite can kill. Not so much since 1981 when they got the antivenom."

"Is that your attempt to know me better?"

"Of course. You said I should ask you things. So I did."

Emma shakes her head and wipes her eyes, choking with glee, as the waiter appears, pushing a cart with the ingredients for his Caesar salad. Emma remembers Hanna's warning: the show is about to begin. But she doesn't care. Her cioppino magically appears before her, and the fragrant steam makes her mouth water. She knows she should wait for his food to be served, but she won't risk missing it again. She grabs a crusty piece of hot baguette and digs in.

CHAPTER 32

That was the most fun dinner in ages, Emma thinks, closing the door to Medical in Frank's face and heading to her cabin. He invited her over for a nightcap, but she declined. So he took her back to her place, but, surprise, surprise, her cabin was behind Medical's locked door, which he didn't have access to.

She's still laughing at the befuddled expression on his face as she crosses the waiting room and opens the door to the staff's quarters. The place is empty and quiet, but the door next to hers is cracked open. Darn, Emma thinks as she tiptoes by without looking in, eager to get into her cabin. No such luck.

"Emma?"

"Yes."

"May I speak to you?"

I should have gone for that nightcap, Emma thinks. But it's too late.

"Sure. What can I do for you?"

"I'd like to chat."

Emma glances at all the doors, wondering if anyone's

listening. Either way, she doesn't want him in her cabin, so she steps in gingerly to a ghostlike Fajar watching some old movie with the sound turned off. He sweeps a pile of clothes from the loveseat to the floor to make room for Emma and kicks the shoe keeping the door open, and the door slams shut.

Emma sighs, wishing she was anywhere but here. It's close to midnight, and she's alone in a cabin with this man she knows nothing about, except that he's the married fiancé of a woman who died a dubious death. Still, she's here.

"What can I do for you, Fajar?"

She can't help but feel sorry for him. This handsome man looks like a relic of himself. Unshaved, red-eyed, and miserable, he's a man in mourning.

"Thank you, Emma. I had to speak to someone and couldn't think of anyone better."

"Sure."

"You know I was Amanda's lover."

"Fiancé, her mother said."

"Yes. And you know I'm married."

Emma nods.

"Amanda knew it too. She was OK with it. She'd met my wife and my kids, and they got along swimmingly."

"How about your wife? Was she OK with it too?"

"As a matter of fact, she was. My wife and I, we are Muslims. In our religion, a man can have up to four wives as long as he can support them and treats them all the same. So I asked my wife's permission to marry Amanda, and she said yes."

What a load of BS, Emma thinks.

"Really?" she asks.

"Yes."

"And what did Amanda say?"

"Amanda said yes. She told me that she'd fallen in love with me, but after meeting my family, she fell in love with them too. She couldn't have children, so she looked forward to being a mother to our kids. She brought them gifts and taught them English. We all looked forward to spending the day together in Semarang.

The idea of Amanda, a beautiful and independent woman choosing to enter a polygamous marriage is baffling for Emma.

"And how was that going to work? Was Amanda going to move to Indonesia?"

"No, she couldn't do that because of her parents. We decided to all move to the US instead. But to marry Amanda under US law, I had to divorce my wife first. On paper only, of course. Then I could marry Amanda and get a Green Card for the kids and me, and after that, we'd bring my wife over. That's why we had to schedule the wedding for next fall. We had to wait for the divorce to go through."

"I see," Emma said, even though she didn't. "But what does that have to do with me?"

"I needed you to understand my situation. As soon as we get to a port, police will come to investigate Amanda's death, and they'll look for a suspect. And I'm the obvious one. I was her lover, and I found the body. They'll think I had a reason to kill her."

"Did you?"

"Of course not. I loved Amanda. Besides that, she was my ticket to get a better life for myself and my family. Why on earth would I kill her?"

"Do you think she killed herself?"

"No."

"Why not?"

"She had no reason to. She was so happy to plan the wedding and looked forward to seeing the kids in Semarang. I know she'd already bought gifts for them, though she didn't tell me what they were since she wanted them to be a surprise. She'd bought a gift for Anissa too — that's my wife. Amanda called her Sister Anissa. Anyhow, I'm sure she didn't commit suicide."

"So if you didn't kill her and she didn't kill herself, what happened?"

"Well, it could have been a freak accident. She could have overdosed by mistake. She may have had an extra glass of wine or given her insulin without her glasses or something. But I don't think that's likely."

"What do you think?"

"I think someone killed her and tried to make it look like suicide. Unless they didn't. They may have tried to blame the death on me."

"Who'd do that? And why?"

Fajar's eyes leave hers, and Emma knows he's about to lie.

"I don't know."

"Any suspicion?"

"I... I'd been with other women before Amanda, of course. What else could I do? I'm a man, and I've been away from home for months. Some of them didn't like it when I... when I focused on Amanda. They hated her. They even hated me.

Emma remembers Hanna's words, "He has Sue eating out of his hand. And they say he loves them and leaves them."

Could it be Sue? She certainly has the knowledge, the access to insulin, and the universal key to enter any cabin.

A thought crosses Emma's mind.

"Were you faithful... to Amanda and your wife?"

Fajar shrugs.

"Of course. Mostly."

"Did you, by any chance, sleep with Gloria, the new singer?"

"Why would you ask that?"

"Somebody pushed her down the stairs the other night trying to break her neck. Did you?"

Fajar shrugs.

"Of course not."

But he averts his eyes, and Emma knows he's lying. And if he lies about this, what else is he lying about? She shakes her head and opens the door.

Somewhere close, a door slams shut.

Somebody knows she was in Fajar's room, and they won't think she was there to talk. They'll think otherwise.

She'd better watch her back.

CHAPTER 33

Fajar was right, of course. A dozen frowning officials in brown uniforms are waiting for the *Sea Horse* on the Lombok pier. As soon as the gangplank is set, they climb aboard, doing their best to look important.

A handful of traditional Indonesian dancers dressed to the nines stand under a purple canopy waiting to greet the visitors. Behind them, the island's green hills project against the azure waters. A graceful string of smaller islands floats like an emerald necklace on the blue sea, making the industrial port look even uglier.

Emma rushes from port to starboard to take pictures. The promenade deck is empty but for the handful of photographers who won't give up trying to catch the rusty cranes and battered cargo boxes in the golden light. Everyone else jams the hallways, impatient to head out to adventure. Not only to Lombok — a beautiful island — but most passengers are on their way to Bali, the highlight of the cruise. They'll spend the night in Bali and get picked up in Tanjung Benoa tomorrow. It's a long trip, and every moment counts, but by the time Emma finished her walk and downed three mugs of coffee, they're still waiting for the announcement to disembark. *It's got to be those officials*, Emma thinks. She heads down to Medical when her pager goes off.

The captain needs her. Now.

This can't be good news. Emma changes course and finds her way to the navigation deck, where an officer allows her into the captain's office, which crawls with unsmiling uniforms.

The captain nods.

"This is Dr. Steele. She declared the death."

A translator introduces her to the officials.

"They want to know what happened."

"She was dead in her cabin. We tried everything, but were unable to bring her back."

"When did she die?"

"I declared the death at 12:23."

"Why did she die?"

"I don't know. She'll need an autopsy."

"We know that. But do you have any suspicions? Any clues?"

"Her blood sugar was infinitesimally low, and she was an insulin-dependent diabetic. I wouldn't be surprised if this was an insulin overdose."

"Suicide, you mean?"

"I don't know."

"Did you notice any signs of violence on the body?"

"No."

"Any signs of struggle in the cabin?"

"No."

"Who found her?"

"Our crew doctor. Dr. Fajar Saputra."

"What was he doing?"

"He was performing CPR, trying to save her life."

"How did he get there?"

"I don't know. You'll have to ask him."

"Bring him over."

The captain bristles.

"Of course. But first, we have to let the passengers disembark. I can't keep them locked in through the whole procedure, especially since there is no evidence of a crime. I have three thousand people raring to go and spend money in Lombok and Bali. If we keep them here, they will get restless, and your people will suffer. And you know that every shopkeeper, taxi driver, and restaurant owner in the islands depends on the dollars these people spend."

"What if one of them is the killer?"

"First, we don't know that there was a crime. We have no evidence of that, and we have a convincing suicide note. Second, this happened in the crew quarters that passengers cannot access. Third, even if they go ashore, where can they go? We're holding their passports on the ship; we herd them around in buses and count them at every stop. If anyone disappears, it will only make your job easier. You'll know who to look for."

The uniforms grunt at each other.

"OK. But the crew stays put."

There goes my chance to see Bali, Emma thinks. But she has no room to complain. She's in better shape than either Amanda or Fajar.

Two policemen bring Fajar in. His handsome face is haggard, and his blue scrubs look slept in. His eyes meet Emma's, asking for help.

"Dr. Saputra?"

"Yes."

"Thank you, Dr. Steele. You are free to go. We'll call you back later."

Emma glances at Fajar. She feels she's abandoning him, but what else can she do? She drags herself to the door. She'll go to the clinic, then go see Amanda's parents. The captain said he was going to disembark them in Bali.

She glances back from the door to see two officers close their handcuffs on Fajar's wrists.

CHAPTER 34

Late for her clinic, as usual, Emma runs down the stairs to Medical. Just as she opens the door, the speakers break into a static cough, then grunt:

"Passengers on shore excursions B1, B2, and B3 may disembark at this time. All others, please wait for your group to be called. Do not congregate in the hallways."

"Finally! They drove me crazy," Marico says. "They kept coming to ask us about the delay like we can read the captain's thoughts!"

Emma nods and calls in her first patient, a young man with a dirty baseball cap and shifty eyes.

"What can I do for you?"

"I... I'm here with my fiancé."

"Yes."

"She's having some discomfort down below."

"I'll be happy to see her anytime."

"She said she'll come this afternoon. But I wanted to speak to you first."

"Yes."

"We were... we were away from each other for a few

months. We just met again at the beginning of the cruise. And I... I had a discharge a couple weeks ago."

"Did you get checked?"

"No. It got better, so I didn't think it mattered. But now that my fiancé has trouble, I wonder if we should get tested."

"Of course."

"But it's important that she doesn't know."

"Doesn't know what?"

"That it's an STD. Can you just treat her without telling her?"

Emma's jaw drops, and she stares at him in disbelief.

"Not tell her that she has an STD? So what do you think I should tell her?"

"Tell her she's got an infection in her urine or something? And just give her the pills?"

"I'm afraid I can't do that. I never lie to my patients."

"But Doctor, you don't understand. You'll break her heart if you tell her. We are getting married in January. We have already sent the invitations. You would destroy our relationship!"

"Me?"

"What she doesn't know won't hurt her. How about telling her she got it from the toilet seat?"

"As I said, I won't lie to my patients. And I'm not the one destroying your relationship. It wasn't me who gave you an STD."

"But you can't tell her. You'll ruin our marriage. Please!"

His handsome face looks at her imploringly. He does his best to look contrite, but there's still the shadow of a smirk. *He thinks he'll talk me into covering for him*, Emma thinks, resisting the temptation to slap him.

"No. Now, if there's nothing else..."

"Thanks for nothing," he says, punching her desk and blasting out the door. A minute later, Marico comes in.

"Everything OK? What happened?"

"He wants me to tell his fiancé she got an STD from the toilet seat, not from him. I said no."

Marico shakes her head.

"Men. By the way, did you see Fajar?"

Emma opens her mouth and then closes it back.

"Not recently. Why?"

"He's late for his clinic. I paged him, but he didn't answer. I don't know whether to have them wait or tell them to return this afternoon."

Emma sighs.

"Why don't I see those who look urgent, and you tell the others to return this afternoon."

"Thanks, Emma."

Emma gives ibuprofen to a sailor who hurt his back lifting an engine and treats the blisters of a cook who spilled hot grease over his arm. The others will return this afternoon. She doesn't know who'll see them now that Fajar got arrested, but it's not her job to spread the news.

As soon as she's done with the clinics, she heads upstairs to see Amanda's parents. She rings the doorbell, and Amanda's mom opens the door dressed in khakis and a jacket. Emma has never seen her wearing anything else but the nightgown, and her heart skips a beat seeing how much she looks like her daughter. Her husband lies in bed with his shoes on, and the room is full of suitcases.

"Good morning."

"Good morning, Doctor. How are you?"

"Well, thank you. How about you? Getting ready to travel?"

"Not at all."

Emma glances at the pile of suitcases. The woman shrugs.

"The captain came by yesterday and told us he made arrangements for us to return to the US. This morning, the stewards got us packed. But we aren't going anywhere."

"How so?"

"Where can we go? And why? This is our home now. We paid for the cruise, and they have no excuse to disembark us against our will. They didn't even bother to ask if we wanted to go. Isn't that so, dear? Do you want to go?"

"Where?"

"Anywhere."

"No."

"Good."

She sits on the bed by her husband, caressing his hand. He smiles, looking into her eyes.

"How will you manage here without Amanda?"

"Just fine. Amanda didn't do quite as much as she thought. She helped with his medications since I can't see that well, and I'm shaky and clumsy, so I have trouble counting the pills. But she was often too busy to come, so I cared for him without her. I will continue to do it."

"For how long?"

"For as long as I can."

She shrugs and crosses her arms in defiance, and Emma can't help but admire her spunk. But she's worried.

Will the captain disembark them against their will? That's unlikely. Dragging a couple of old people kicking and screaming off the ship would make for bad PR. So what will he do?

That's easy. He'll have Emma do it. He'll ask her to document that they lack decision-making capacity, and he'll have them disembarked on stretchers.

"You have no other children? Close relatives? Friends?"

"No children but Amanda. And at our age, most friends are dead; those who aren't can barely look after themselves. We have nowhere to go but a nursing home, and I know they won't take us together. He needs care 24/7, and I don't. They'll place him in a nursing home and send me to assisted living, and that will be the end of him. He'll be disoriented and distraught. He knows nobody but me and no home other than this cabin."

"I'm so sorry."

"Sorry is not good enough; we need help. Will you help us, Doctor? Please?"

She takes Emma's hand, looking at her with tears in her eyes, and Emma's heart breaks.

"How can I help you?"

"Don't let them send us away."

CHAPTER 35

What a terrible day, and it's not even noon yet, Emma thinks. The only good news is that the ship is as empty as a haunted house. The passengers are gone, but the crew had to stay on board, and they're not happy. Every time they're in port, they can't wait to get off and go to the beach, shop for presents, or at least hang out in the cruise terminals to take advantage of the free internet to FaceTime their loved ones. The internet-at-sea is as slow as it is expensive, even with their discounted internet cards.

Emma lies in her dark, cold cabin, wondering what to do with herself. She tries to read, but the cabin walls feel like they're closing around her, so she decides to do something she hasn't done since setting foot on the ship: She puts on her swimsuit and heads to the pool.

On sea days, the pool is the life center of the ship. As soon as they wake up, passengers drop their towels to claim the lounge chairs. They spend their day there, reading, eating, listening to the live band at noon, and sleeping in the sun until they turn red like cooked lobsters. It's standing room only by ten.

The shore days are a different proposition. It's just the long-timers who partake of the quietude and the blue water: the officers, the long cruisers, and her.

Emma drops her striped towel on the chair closest to the pool and hides her phone and pager underneath. The cool water feels good on her sunburned skin, and she swims laps, happy to be here and alone. She counts ten laps, stops to check her phone and pager, and then dives in to swim another ten. Now that she finally has time to think, she wonders how Taylor is doing. She doesn't email often and doesn't say much when she does. "I took Hope to the pediatrician; they say she's growing well." "The physics professor is a bore." "The weather's getting worse, and I need to buy new boots."

Taylor is hard enough to figure out when they're together; her emails tell Emma nothing about Taylor's ongoing inner troubles. Because Taylor has been troubled since she was a child. Her ups and downs are a wonder to behold; she can go from sky-high to the lowest low at the drop of a hat for no discernible reason. As a teenager, she kept getting in trouble, and Emma had to save her again and again.

But motherhood, as unplanned as it was, gave Taylor a compass by giving her someone else to think about besides herself. Hopefully, her love for Hope will keep her focused and sane.

Emma goes back to check her pager and finds Frank lying in the chair next to hers in a navy Speedo swimsuit that leaves very little to the imagination. He's well-toned and tan, and Emma grabs her towel to cover herself before he gets a chance to have a good look.

"Good morning," he says.

"Anything but that."

He laughs and takes off his dark glasses.

"See, Emma, and you accuse me of being too direct. You can't even say hello properly."

"What are you doing here?"

"Lying in the sun. You?"

"How come you didn't leave the ship to visit the island?"

"I've seen it before. And I'm going tomorrow. How about you?"

"I'm crew. They didn't let me out."

"That's a shame. Why?"

"There are... there are some issues with the Indonesian officials."

"I know. Amanda's death."

"How do you know?"

"Everyone knows. Do you think you can keep something like that a secret? The crew speaks about nothing else. They say her boyfriend killed her."

"Why?"

"He got tired of her, but she wouldn't let go."

"How would they know that?"

"Emma, this is a small ship. Everybody knows everybody else. Somebody will see you no matter where you go and what you do."

"Did you know Amanda?"

"Of course."

"Did you like her?"

"She was beautiful, talented, funny, and kind. What's not to like? She was a lovely woman in and out. And a friend. Her death has been a huge blow."

Something in the way he speaks about Amanda gives Emma pause.

"Were you..."

"Lovers? Of course. For a while. Then she met that young whippersnapper and fell for him like a ton of bricks. I would have been happy to share her attentions, but she said no. It was love, with the big L, she said, and she had no use for me anymore."

"I'm sorry."

"Me too. But life goes on. Not for her, unfortunately. How did she die?"

"I thought you knew everything."

"Of course. Some say he cut her throat with a machete. Others say he poisoned her. But the big money is on him choking her as they made love. They say she was into kinky sex and that it was an accident. Which one is true?"

"I don't know. I don't think he killed her."

"Why not?"

"He doesn't look like a killer to me."

"What do you know about killers?"

"More than I'd like to. So tell me about Bali."

"How about I take you there tomorrow?"

"Sure. If they let me off the ship."

"Let me pull some strings. See if I can get you out."

"Thanks."

He won't be able to, of course, since the whole crew is consigned to the ship, but he's nice to try. Emma thinks he's a fascinating guy, but something about the way he spoke about Amanda leaves her unsettled. Even more, something about the way he talked about Fajar. It's like he wants him to be guilty.

CHAPTER 36

That afternoon, Emma oversaw her own clinic, then Fajar's. She wasn't surprised when she got called by the captain. She'd been expecting it earlier, but he must have been busy.

Behind his mahogany desk, with the setting sun throwing deep shade on his face, the captain looked years older than the last time he invited Emma for a talk.

"Thanks for coming. Please sit. I need your help."

"With?"

"The cruise director's parents don't want to leave the ship."

"Yes."

"I need you to get them out."

"Me?"

"Yes. They're both demented and unable to care for themselves. They can't stay on the ship. The company made arrangements for them to fly home tomorrow."

"Home where?"

"To New York. A company representative will wait for them there and redirect them."

"To where?"

"To wherever they belong. I don't know, and that's not my problem. My problem is that I need them off the ship, and they don't want to leave. I need you to medically disembark them."

"What for?"

"They're demented. They can't care for themselves here."

"Dementia is not an emergency medical condition. They were just as demented last week and the week before that. To disembark them, I need a medical emergency. And even then, I don't think I could do it if they don't want to leave."

The captain's irritation is apparent in his voice.

"But they are demented. They don't understand, so they don't have a choice."

"Actually, I spent some time with them this morning. The lady is completely lucid. She understands exactly what is happening, and she wants to stay on the ship. There's nothing I could do if I wanted to. And I don't."

"Dr. Steele, it pains me to tell you that what you want and what you don't want is less important to me than the ship's well-being. We can't afford to babysit them. It was bad enough when Amanda was here to look after them. She often passed their care to the staff, who are busy enough with their jobs. Now that she's gone, there's nobody to take care of them. It's in their best interest to go someplace where they'll be safe. They aren't safe here. What if they wander away or fall down the stairs or even overboard? How will you feel about your refusal to keep them safe?"

"Not good, I'm sure, but that hasn't happened yet. And I have no justification for making decisions on their behalf. And neither have you."

"Come on! It's so easy! Just sign the damned paperwork

and give them something to keep them quiet as they disembark! If they understood what's happening, they'd be grateful."

"No."

"That's it then. Don't expect me to do you any favors."

Emma laughs.

"I don't. What happened with the search for the cause of the sickness of Amanda's parents and the other three cabins? Did you ever find anything?"

"Of course not. There was nothing to find."

"Of course."

Back in her cabin, Emma opens her wine. She considers drinking it straight from the bottle rather than bothering with the mug, where she can't even see its color. But no. It's bad enough that she drinks this sorry excuse for wine when she should stay sober and keep her head clear.

She empties the mug and pours another when somebody knocks at the door.

"Who is it?"

"Fajar."

Fajar? Isn't he in jail?

Emma opens the door, and Fajar slips in. He's wearing the same tired scrubs he wore this morning, and he looks like he's drowning. As much as she's unsure what to think about him, Emma feels sorry for him.

"Sit."

Emma pours the rest of the wine into a second mug and hands it to him. He empties it in one gulp.

"Thanks."

Emma nods.

"Thank you for taking care of my clinic. I'll be glad to take care of yours if you want to get off the ship tomorrow."

"I can't. The crew stays in."

"You're not crew. You're somewhere in no man's land, not quite crew, but not a passenger either. The captain may let you go if you ask him.

"I'd be surprised," Emma said, remembering their conversation. "He doesn't like me much."

"Why?"

"He wanted me to medically disembark Amanda's parents, and I said no. He wasn't pleased."

"Why? Are they sick?"

"He doesn't think they can make it on their own, and they'll be a burden to the crew."

"He may have a point. But that's not a reason to disembark them now."

"Thank you. How did you escape? I thought they arrested you."

"They did, but the captain didn't let them take me. They had no proof of any kind, and he didn't want to be a doctor short on the ship. He told them he won't let me off the ship and they could find me here anytime. They'll autopsy Amanda's body and get back to me. We're still in Indonesian waters for almost a week. They can pick me up any time."

"How are you doing?"

"Lousy. I'm scared and pissed, but at least it takes my mind off Amanda's death."

He laughs, and Emma can't help but smile at his charm.

"OK. I'll go try to get some sleep now," he continues. "Hopefully, with the ship half empty since so many went to Bali, they won't need us tonight."

His hand on the door, he turns to Emma.

"I don't think it was the insulin."

"Why not?"

"I don't think she killed herself. And insulin would have been impossible to give without her noticing. I also just found out that I'm missing a bottle of glipizide. It would be easy to crush the pills and give them to her in a drink or in food. Alternatively, someone drugged her and then injected her with insulin.

That makes sense, Emma thinks.

"Who would do that?"

Fajar shrugs.

"I don't know. But whoever it is, I'll find out and make them pay."

He leaves, and Emma wonders why he came to see her tonight. To thank her? He could have done that in the morning. To persuade her that he's innocent? But why, unless he happened to be guilty? Or maybe to provoke whoever killed Amanda and pushed Gloria down the stairs to have a go at her, Emma. Is he using her as bait?

CHAPTER 37

The following morning, Emma's brushing her teeth when the cabin phone rings.

"Yes?"

"Get ready. I'm taking you out for the day."

"You're what?"

"I'm taking you out for the day. I spoke to the captain, and he'll let you go. I'll meet you at the gangplank in half an hour."

Somewhat skeptical, Emma throws her sunscreen, her bug repellant, and a bottle of water in a light pack. She puts on a dress and a hat and gets to the gangplank just as Frank arrives.

"You look good for how fast you got ready."

"Thanks. I think."

"It's a compliment. I once had a wife who took an hour to put on makeup to get to the mailbox. It was all worth it. You didn't want to see her when she woke up."

Emma presents her ID to the security officer for scanning, half expecting to be told she can't leave the boat. She's wrong.

"Have a good day, doctor. You too, sir."

Emma looks at Frank, her eyes wide.

"How did you make this happen?"

"I spoke to the captain. I had to beat him up, but he said yes."

Emma laughs.

"I'm kidding, of course. He actually seemed pleased to get rid of you. 'Show her a good time,' he said. We aren't leaving until midnight."

"Really!"

"Yep. What did you do to him?"

"I refused him a favor."

"Do that more often. That seems to improve his mood."

Their Jeep is waiting on the pier.

"Another friend?"

"Not this time. I hired a guide. There's so much to see and so little time. What do you know about Bali?"

"It's an island. They have great dancers."

"That's it? You're in for a treat."

The driver is a handsome Indian man in his thirties with a blinding white smile. He opens the door and welcomes them with clipped, fast words that sound like marbles rolling down stone stairs.

"Welcome! My name is Nyoman, but you can call me Man. That means the third since I'm the third son of my family. In Bali, we name our children by birth order. The eldest is Wayan, the second is Made, then Nyoman. The fourth one would be Ketut."

"What happens if a family has more than four children?" Frank asked.

"They start over. The fifth will be "Wayan Balik, Wayan again. We're not very inventive with our names, but that leaves more creativity for other things. You're about to see some of that soon in the Ubud Markets. After that, I'll take you to the Goa Gajah temple and the rice terraces of Tegallalang. Then we'll go to the Tannah Lot Temple to see the sunset and a traditional Balinese dance. OK?"

"Phenomenal."

"Good. Relax and enjoy."

Man merges into traffic, zig-zagging between zippy scooters and rusty cars fixed with tape. Frank takes Emma's hand.

"How have you been?"

Shocked by the touch and the question, Emma nods.

"OK. You?"

"Better now that you're here. I miss Amanda. You remind me of her."

"How so?"

"You're beautiful, direct, and spunky. And you don't put up with any shit. But enough of that. Let me tell you about Bali. Most people don't know it, but Bali is not a country. It's just one of Indonesia's thousands of islands. But unlike most Indonesians, who are Muslims, the Balinese are Hindu. Until the Dutch colonized them in 1906, Bali was an independent kingdom. The Japanese needed a good port, so they occupied them during the Second World War. Then the allies threw out the Japanese, and Bali became part of Indonesia."

"Complicated history," Emma says.

Frank nods. "It is, isn't it? The island is shaped like a chicken looking sideways, about 95 miles wide and 70 miles long. It has a bunch of active volcanoes that channel the rain and fertilize the soil. That may be why they boast one of the world's highest biodiversities of marine species. Bali has seven times more coral than the Caribbean."

"Very impressive for a non-Balinese, sir," Man says and parks the Jeep.

The narrow streets choke with stalls loaded with everything from sandals to statues. Smiling vendors praise their wares, and women with jet-black hair tied into low ponytails walk gracefully under the weight of the bundles and boxes they carry on their heads. The smell of coffee competes with the rotten stench of durian, and it loses.

Man stops by a woman selling food and buys a bag of unidentifiable brown blobs that he offers to Emma.

"That's our traditional *jaja klepon*. Palm-sugar filled gelatinous balls rolled in grated coconut."

Emma wishes she could refuse, but she can't. But, once you get over the jellyfish texture, they are delicious. She offers them to Frank, but he shakes his head. Emma picks another one and devours it with relish just to show him.

Endless rows of stalls bend under the weight of merchandise of all sorts. Traditional Bali rattan bags — square and round, big and small, white and black, and everything in between — rub shoulders with baskets, platters, and everything else rattan.

Wood carvings pile high on rugs set on the ground: fish-shaped wooden platters, cutting boards carved from a whole tree trunk with the wood rings shining through, salad bowls you could bathe in, mortars and pestles for crushing spices, eating utensils fit for giants.

Macrame stands sport plant hangers and pastel-colored dream catchers with white feathers fluttering in the breeze. Jewelry stands with simple silver bracelets and complicated snake-shaped rings in rainbow colors. Hand-made leather wallets and belts, and shoes.

Then the clothes: fine Batik sarongs in every color from water-turquoise to bold coral, blood red, and dark purple hang next to summer dresses and shirts with complicated ikat patterns.

Emma checks out the sarongs.

"You have to bargain," Man says.

Emma chooses a red one with white fish skeletons for herself and a green one with rice fields for Taylor. She takes out her wallet, but Man takes over.

"You can't pay full price, or you'll look like a tourist!"

Emma laughs, but Man is not kidding. He starts a heated debate with the woman. She pretends to burst into tears and shakes the sarongs in his face to demonstrate their quality, but Man doesn't relent. Five minutes later, Emma gets her sarongs at half price.

She shrugs and buys another purple one for Margret and a yellow one for Amber, who is blonde and hates yellow, and pays. Man looks at her in distress.

"Are you kidding? If I knew you wanted four, I could get them cheaper!"

Frank laughs and helps her to the car. The next stop is the Goa Gajah temple inside a cave.

"The legend says the giant Kebo Iwa made it by digging into the cliff with his fingernail," Man says. "But archeologists think it dates from the eleventh century Bali Kingdom since it contains both Buddhist and Hindu imagery. The faces carved in stone are meant to ward off evil spirits. The primary figure may have been an elephant, hence the nickname Elephant Cave."

Emma studies the countless evil faces grimacing at her from the rock and wonders what about its ugliness makes it sacred. They walk in under the trunkless elephant crowning the opening who stares at them with bulbous eyes. The cave inside is smoky with incense and crammed with tourists wrapped in rented sarongs who make fun of each other.

"Here, like in all Bali temples, visitors must wear modest attire. Menstruating women are not allowed in."

What's with these people and their menstruation obsession? Emma wonders, remembering Komodo. *But maybe it's not menstruation they have a problem with; it's womanhood.*

The drive north is exhilarating. The undulating rice terraces of Tegallalang follow each other like waves in a sea of green that lasts as far as the eye can see. The rice plants are so green they don't look real. Water drops scatter the sunlight, softening the shades of green to please the eye and touch the soul with softness. So far away that he looks like a child's toy, a farmer with a conical hat carries a pole with two woven baskets balanced at each end.

Emma drinks in the beauty and takes picture after picture.

"This is one of the most beautiful places I've ever seen."

Frank agrees. "I've never seen something so green."

"It's our irrigation system. The Subak irrigation system was designated a World Heritage Site. A thousand years ago, our ancestors built a whole ecosystem consisting of terraced rice fields, forests protecting the water supply, water canals, and temples. Bali has more than a thousand water collectives where hundreds of farmers share the same water supply."

Emma is sad to leave the green paradise, but the clock is ticking. She'll soon have to be back on the boat, and the thought makes her shiver. Feeling her unease, Frank touches her shoulder, and Emma feels grateful. As awkward as he is, he's the closest thing she's got to a friend.

It's close to midnight when Emma finally gets to her cabin after an exhausting but satisfying day. Frank may be a little on the autism spectrum, but he's the best travel partner she's ever had — quiet, inexhaustible, and funny. Next time he wants to take her somewhere, she'll say yes.

It's dark and quiet in Medical as Emma tiptoes through her door. She drops her shopping on the sofa and heads to the bathroom for a shower.

Something doesn't feel right. But what?

The shower is empty and dry. The soap is where she left it. The sink. The toilet. Nothing unusual.

It's the shampoo. It sits on its base. She always sets it upside down since she's too impatient to wait for it to flow. Somebody turned it right side up.

But why? And who?

She steps back into the room and sees more subtle signs. Her roll-on peeks from under the bed. The closet door is not closed all the way.

She checks the fridge. Three bottles of water, closed. A stale cheese sandwich she saved for the 2 a.m. munchies. Two-thirds of a dark chocolate bar. A bottle of white wine.

She checks it carefully. Somebody fooled with the cork's metal cover, and they didn't do a clean job.

She takes off the cover to study the cork. It looks fine.

She gets her doctor's bag and finds the magnifier she uses for the tiny splinters too small to see with the naked eye. There's a microscopic hole in the cork. Somebody stuck a needle in it. Why? To add something to the wine, of course. What else did they fool around with?

She throws away the wine, the shampoo, the food, and the toothpaste. The only thing she can't bring herself to throw away is her eye drops bottle. Her dry eyes will kill her without them. But she throws away the drops and rinses the bottle before filling it with water from the tap.

CHAPTER 38

Emma's clinic is busy this morning. The passengers who returned from their overnight trip to Bali need lots of love. Between sunburns, sprains, and indigestions, Emma doesn't have time to worry about anything else, and by the time she gets a break, it's time for lunch.

She decides to try the crew mess rather than dress up to go upstairs. The place is almost empty since the crew's busy running around to take care of the passengers' needs.

Emma gets in line behind two sailors and watches them get rice, then fill their plates with chunks of meat swimming in a thick black gravy.

"What's that?" she asks.

The men shrug.

"Rawon. It's a beef stew from East Java. It's black because of the keluak nuts that give it a nutty flavor. Add shallots, turmeric, and red chili, and you'll get what they call rawon setan in Surabaya. That's Devil's soup," Fajar says, lining up behind her. "How was your day yesterday?"

"Fantastic. Thank you for taking my clinic and making it possible."

"No problem. Not many patients, anyhow. They were too busy to be sick. I bet it's different today."

"Yes."

Emma pours rawon over her rice and sits at the table in the corner. Fajar joins her moments later.

"How about your day?" Emma asks.

Fajar shrugs.

"It was uneventful, but for one thing."

"What?"

"The captain asked me to disembark Amanda's parents."

"I knew it! That's why he was glad to have me off the ship. Did you?"

"No."

"What did he say?"

"Nothing pleasant."

"I bet."

Emma dips her spoon in the rawon, and the black gravy coats her spoon like thick mud. Not the kind of food she's used to, but she can't just throw it away. She smells it. Garlic, ginger, and something else she can't name. She licks the tip of the spoon and digs in. The black stew is spicy, hot, and delicious.

"This is good."

"It's my favorite dish. Yesterday after clinic, I went to see Amanda's parents. I hadn't dared see them before because I didn't know what to say, and I was afraid I'd only hurt them more. But they were pleased to see me. Especially her mom."

"How are they managing?"

"They seem OK. They're glad to be on the ship and together. Amanda's dad doesn't seem to remember her, but her mom does, of course. We talked about her, and it was bittersweet. I promised I'd help her take care of him. I'll set up his meds and help her bathe him. While I'm still here."

Emma remembers that Fajar is on borrowed time. They could come after him any day.

"That's kind of you."

"That's the one thing I can do for Amanda."

"You miss her?"

"Very much."

"She sounds like an extraordinary person."

"She was. She was bright, engaging, and fun. She always managed to find the silver lining, as you Americans say. I still can't believe she's dead. I haven't even told my wife yet. She'll be devastated."

Emma pushes her empty plate to the side.

"You know, Fajar, I find it hard to understand the complicated relationship between you, your wife, and Amanda."

Fajar shrugs.

"That's because you are a Western woman. It's not complicated at all. It's, in fact, very simple. Like me, my wife grew up in her father's house with her mother and his other two wives. To her, having sister wives is normal. Useful, in fact. My mothers shared childcare and chores, and they sat together drinking tea and complaining about their husband like all women do. They shared a kinship."

"Weren't they jealous of each other?"

"Occasionally. But my father took great care to show no preference for any of his wives. Whatever he felt inside, he never showed it to them. They each had their nights with him — my mother had Mondays and Thursdays, my mother Alli had Tuesdays and Saturdays, and my mother Inna had Wednesdays and Sundays."

"What happened on Fridays?"

"Friday is the holy day for us Muslims. On Fridays, Father slept in his own bed."

Emma has a hard time wrapping her mind around this arrangement.

"Emma, marriage is not just sex. It's a family, a community, and an economic unit. It functions much better when you have more than two people butting heads."

"Who made the decisions?"

"My father was supposed to. But really, it was the women. Once they agreed on something, he could do nothing but go along with it. He was a minority."

"Did they usually agree?"

"Almost always."

"And when they didn't?"

"They talked it through until they found a compromise."

"But how did Amanda ever get into this? She wasn't brought up Muslim. How could she accept this?"

"When Amanda and I became lovers, it was all about sex. She knew I was married and had kids, but they were too far away to matter. Then, when we fell in love and started thinking about a long-term relationship, I told her I would never leave my wife. Not only do I love her, but she's the mother of my children and my responsibility. So, with my wife's permission, I asked Amanda to join us. If you think about it, she already had. She said yes."

Emma shakes her head. This is logical and makes perfect sense, but it goes against Emma's every instinct.

Fajar laughs.

"You must have been an only child."

"Yes."

"See, that's part of the problem. As an only child, you never learned to share the love. All firstborns have trouble seeing their parents fall in love with their younger siblings.

Still, they eventually learn there's enough love to go around. Only children don't get to learn that lesson. You just never learned to share your parents' love."

Emma sighs.

"Fajar, this time, you've got it wrong. I would have gladly shared everything my mother had for me."

There wasn't much love. But there were plenty of other things.

CHAPTER 39

The evening clinic was just as bad as the morning one. After two long days in Bali, most passengers chose to stay on the ship and get help for their insomnia, chronic constipation, and five years' worth of elbow pain.

Still, Emma enjoyed spending time with them, and being with people gave her comfort. Because deep inside, she was worried. Whoever broke into her cabin and fooled with her wine meant her no good. She tried to tell herself that she was being paranoid. Maybe it was the steward coming to take the trash — though they never did. Or perhaps somebody was looking for something worth stealing, like cash or an expensive camera. But nothing was missing. And all the terrible things that had happened made Emma wary. It was like an evil spirit haunted the ship. But Emma didn't believe in ghosts, evil or otherwise, and she felt endangered. It made her uncomfortable to be alone.

Emma went to her cabin and locked the door as soon as the clinic was over. She had just started an email to Margret when the phone rang.

"Hello."

"Long time no see. How are you doing, Emma?"

"I'm good. How are you, Hanna?"

"OK. How about meeting me for a drink at the Club? There's somebody I'd like you to meet."

"Sure. Where is it?"

"Ninth deck. Don't tell me you haven't yet scoped all the spots on the ship."

"I've been a little busy."

"I bet. See you there in half an hour."

Emma put on her eternal black dress, promising herself to buy another next time she gets ashore. She slicked on some lipstick, threw her phone and pager in her bag, and took the stairs to the Club. She could certainly use the exercise, since between the all-you-can-eat buffets, the stress, and the lack of exercise, she has gained weight, which is the last thing she needs. She's never been slim, but these last few weeks have damaged her.

She hasn't been around the ship much in the evenings, and it's nice to see the decked-out couples enjoying themselves. And they're all couples: sitting by the pool listening to Gloria and the band playing Harry Belafonte, browsing the shelves with fragrances and designer bags, listening to the vendors' pitch on how emeralds and pearls are not an expense but a worthwhile investment, or sipping from tall frosty glasses with little umbrellas.

Looking smashing in her sea-green silk dress, Hanna waves from a round table by the piano.

"There you are. Come sit. What do you want to drink?"

"Hi, Hanna. I'll take a dry martini."

"Gin or vodka?"

"Gin."

"Of course." Hanna signals a waiter who stops to drop a bowl of assorted warm nuts and take their order.

"Eddie, we'll have two Hendricks martinis extra dry with three olives and a twist."

"Certainly."

Emma's eyes follow the Asian waiter.

"Is his name really Eddie?"

Hanna laughs.

"Of course not. The crew working directly with the public adopts Western nicknames. It's easier for the passengers to remember and pronounce them. And it seems to bring higher tips."

"But isn't it awful that they must give up their own name?"

"That's what I thought too, but then I asked some crew friends. They said they prefer it that way. It protects their privacy, so they can keep their real name for their friends."

"I hadn't thought about it that way."

"Of course not. Like me, you're an outsider. Developing relationships takes time. By the way, how are you doing with your friend Sue?"

"Much better. I barely ever see her."

"Yeah, I heard she's struggling.

"How did you hear?"

"Through the grapevine. My cabin steward is good friends with the steward who cleans Medical. He heard the whole fight, and he said it wasn't pretty. They shouted and called each other ugly names while he mopped, so he stopped and listened. What else could he do? Plus, the more hot gossip he's got, the more everybody fights to buy him drinks at the crew bar."

"Wow. I didn't know it was that bad. I wonder how they manage to work together after that."

"Work together? What are you talking about?"

"Well, Sue is the lead nurse, and Fajar is the crew doc. They have no other choice but to work together."

"What does Fajar have to do with it?"

"Didn't you just say they fought and called each other names?"

"Not Fajar. Will. He and Sue fought like cats and dogs. Then Will apparently had enough. He disembarked in Bali and never came back."

"Really?"

"That's what they said. I'm wondering how he got his passport, though. The office folks love to hold on to them. That ensures that the crew can't just disappear and leave the ship short-staffed. But Will isn't crew, of course. As Sue's husband, he straddles the line between passenger and crew. He's neither one nor the other. Or both. Depending on how you choose to see it."

Eddie brings the martinis. Hanna slips him a banknote.

"We'll take another set when I wave to you," she says.

He bows and leaves. Hanna lifts her frosted triangular glass.

"Cheers. To better days for everybody. Or if not for everybody, at least for the two of us."

"I'll drink to that."

The frozen martini bursts with flavors. The lemon scent and the briny taste of the olives mingle with the aroma of the juniper infused with rose and cucumber.

"Am I late?"

With her amber slanted eyes and skin like forest honey, the woman would be spectacular anytime, anywhere. But on this ship of retired Westerners, she glows like a full moon in a dark sky. Every eye in the bar is glued to the red dress that looks sewn on her and her shiny black hair falling to her low back. But her eyes are on Emma.

"Khun Nok. So good to see you. Meet my friend Emma."

"So glad to meet you, Emma. What are you guys drinking?"

"Martinis. What would you like, Nok?"

"I'll have a Mai Tai. I haven't had one in forever."

Her voice is low and throaty, making her accent even sexier.

Hanna waves. Eddie nods and gets busy.

"I've never had a Mai Tai," Emma says. What is it?"

"White rum, lime juice, Curacao, dark rum with lime peel, and a pineapple spear. But it's essential to float the dark rum on top."

"Why?"

Nok shrugs.

"Who knows? Most likely just the PR. 'Cause it surely doesn't change the taste."

Emma laughs and wonders who this is. One of the dancers, maybe?

"But honestly, the whole Mai Tai thing is just a PR stunt. Thai people don't drink that. They just sell it to naïve Farangs. Actually, I changed my mind. I'll have a Sabai-Sabai instead. I love the aroma of Thai basil with lemon."

She turns to Emma.

"So good to meet you, Emma. My husband told me a lot about you."

"He did?"

"Yes. I have to admit he was pissed. That made me even more eager to meet you. 'She's not feminine,' he said. 'She expects to be respected like a man.' He hates that, you know. I love it, of course."

"Oh. I don't remember meeting your husband."

"Oh, but you did. Captain Pieter van Huis. I'm his wife."

CHAPTER 40

Emma's jaw falls. She stares at the bombshell looking like a movie star who must be two decades younger than her husband, and looks for words.

"You aren't the kind of wife I thought he'd have."

Hanna and Nok choke with laughter, and Emma tries to recuperate.

"Sorry. That sounds awful. I just meant that the captain looks so straight and narrow; I thought he'd have a sturdy Dutch wife and at least seven kids. And you don't look like that."

Nok glances at Hanna and laughs.

"You were right. She's just like you said. Thanks for having us meet." She turns to Emma and lifts her glass. "Here's to the beginning of a splendid relationship."

"Thanks, I think."

"Of course. Pieter is a little stiff, but then how can he help it? This fucking ship is a hard master. He can never relax. He's a different man when he's on vacation, but sadly he's very seldom on vacation. So, every once in a while, much to my chagrin, I join him on the ship. Sometimes he notices I'm here, and sometimes he does not. But what's a good little wife to do? I have to stand by my man."

Eddie comes with the drinks. Nok sits on the sofa next to Emma and lifts her glass.

"*Chok dee.* That's Thai for cheers. To a lovely friendship."

"Cheers."

Nok sniffs her cloudy frosted glass sprouting a twig of basil, and smiles. She takes a sip and leans back, checking the crowd. Her heart-shaped face glows like she's lit from the inside. She must be the most beautiful woman I've ever met, Emma thinks. In her drab black dress, she feels like a chicken next to a peacock. And what's even worse is that she really likes the peacock.

"Are you Thai?" she asks.

"Of course. Pieter and I met in Phuket, and we stayed in touch. Then, when he needed a wife, we got married."

"Why did he need a wife?"

"For various reasons, one being that it's hard to get promoted unless you are happily married. The cruise companies are still very conventional. They pay lip service to diversity and all that. Still, in reality, they don't have a single captain who is black, female, or openly gay."

"You miss Thailand?"

"I make sure I don't. I never leave it for too long. I plan to disembark in Bangkok and go home."

"Where's home?"

"Up north, in the mountains. Chiang Mai. It's the second largest city in Thailand, and it's more than seven hundred years old, surrounded by old brick walls and a deep moat. But it's still a village at heart. You can walk everywhere, and there's always someone who knows someone who can make things happen for you."

"It sounds wonderful."

"It is. I'll take you there someday. But tell me about you. Are you married?"

"Divorced."

"Good. American?"

"Yes."

"Well, that's not your fault. How do you like being on the ship?"

Emma chokes. What can she say to that?

"It takes some getting used to."

Nok laughs and waves to Eddie for another drink.

"Sue's poisoning your life, isn't she?"

"She's doing her best."

"Why? Is Fajar hitting on you?"

Emma blushes.

"Of course not."

"Why? He hits on everything with two legs, even the painting ladder, unless they have a dick. He hasn't met a woman he didn't want to bed."

"Really?"

"Absolutely. Is that right, Hanna?"

"Of course."

"Did he hit on you too?" Emma asks.

"A little."

Emma feels abandoned. Fajar has never hit on her. Or did he?

"He never hit on me."

"Maybe he was busy with Amanda's death and everything. Don't worry; he will. Just don't take him seriously. He's all for one-night stands."

"How about Amanda?"

"Amanda was his door to a Green Card and getting to the U.S. That's worth a little boredom."

"You don't think he loved her?"

"Sure he did. Just not enough to be faithful to her. But I'm sure he was pissed when she died. Made his plans fall apart."

"How do you know he wasn't faithful to Amanda?"

Nok laughs so hard that her lovely amber eyes tear up.

"I can't tell you here and now, Emma. But trust me, I do."

Her smile speaks volumes, implying that she has first-hand knowledge of Fajar's trysts. But really? On this ship where her husband is the captain, and everybody knows everything about everybody?

Nok reads her mind.

"Just because they know it doesn't mean they have to talk. And if they do, they take care who they speak to."

"So you don't think he killed her?" Hanna asks.

"Not really, though I heard she was getting really clingy. They had a couple of nasty fights when she learned about his escapades. But I wouldn't think he'd kill her and give up the hope for an American passport."

She drains her glass and sets it on the table.

"I'm sorry to leave you, ladies, but I need to entertain some of my husband's very boring guests, and I can't be late. That's one of the few demands he makes of me. But I look forward to seeing you really soon, Emma." Her warm hand squeezes Emma's fingers, and her eyes hold Emma's a second longer than necessary.

"Give me a call when you have time. I can't wait to chat about Fajar and Amanda. Other things too."

As she leaves, every eye in the bar stays glued to her red dress, cut so low in the back that it shows the dimples above her buttocks.

"She's something else," Hanna says.

"She sure is, but I'm not sure what."

"She's a confident, sensual, and beautiful woman who doesn't care what others think about her."

"I wish I was like that," Emma says.

"Sure you do. Everybody does. You might be someday, but for now, you're pretty good the way you are."

"I wish I felt that way." Emma shrugged.

"You wouldn't be you if you did. You never feel good enough, smart enough, and accomplished enough; that's why you always try harder. That's one of your most endearing features."

"Thanks, Hanna. But I'd switch with Nok in a heartbeat."

"You don't know what you're talking about, but you'll find out someday. In the meantime, keep being you."

CHAPTER 41

Emma stands at the bow on the *Sea Horse's* ninth deck to take pictures of the fast-approaching port of Semarang. Frank told her that at almost two million people, Semarang is one of the largest cities in Indonesia, and it was declared the cleanest city in South Asia. Emma takes in the long concrete pier and the murky water and wonders how.

Still, this stop is unique. Covered with people dressed in bright colors carrying balloons and flowers, the long skinny pier looks like a garden. After months of separation, the Indonesian crew's families have come to visit their loved ones, and the joy of the reunion brightens every face.

As soon as the passengers finish disembarking, a rainbow-colored human wave floods the gangplank. The decks are chock-full of grinning sailors waving and shouting to call their families. They're all dressed to the nines: Smiling women with bright flowers in their dark hair hold the hands of little girls in ruffled dresses with arms full of flowers. Serious little boys importantly carry armfuls of balloons.

As soon as they see their fathers, the kids let go of their

mothers' hands to rush into their arms. The women smile with tears in their eyes.

"Isn't it touching?" Frank asks.

He lifts his microwave-sized camera to take Emma's picture.

"It is. Don't take my picture."

"Why not? You're afraid I'll steal your soul?"

"Nope. But I wish I had put on lipstick and worn something else besides the darn scrubs. I wish I looked glamorous and cool."

"But you're not glamorous and cool."

"I know. But you don't have to say it."

"You're real, natural, and full of life. That's better than glamorous and cool."

Emma flicks her hand to dismiss him and returns to the joyful family reunions six decks below. She lives vicariously through their joy, knowing that if her own family visited, it wouldn't be anything like this. Taylor would nod politely if she was having a good day and glare like an evil spirit if she wasn't. Little Hope is too young to recognize her. As for Victor, he now belongs to Amber.

"They look so happy to meet their families it's hard to believe that they all have 'ship spouses,'" Frank says.

"Do they?"

"Of course. Different ship spouses on different contracts. Couples break apart and change partners at the end of each contract. What can they do? They live on a ship for four months, go home for two, then return on a different ship to start over, and they do that for years. It's a lifestyle."

"How do you know this?"

"Emma, I've practically lived on ships for the last three years. I met the same people over and over, and we became friends."

Emma sighs. "It's sad, really. They don't get to see their children grow up, and their spouses are only part-time."

"It's a choice. Their families live better lives thanks to the money they earn. They get to see the world. Most of them do it for a few years, enough to build up a little nest egg at home, then return to their normal lives. And having a part-time spouse isn't that bad. Better than getting on each other's nerves all the time. You get to enjoy being together again. I might have never gotten divorced if I was only part-time married."

"Tell me about your wives."

Frank shrugs.

"I was still in college when I met my first wife. We dated for a few years, then we got married because everybody else around us did. She needed constant validation that she was the prettiest wife, the best cook, and the most successful teacher. But she was none of that, and I wouldn't lie to her. Even the sex became boring when we didn't have to steal it anymore. So she found someone who lied better, and I felt grateful. I still send him Christmas cards."

"How about the second wife?"

"I stayed single for a few years. Then I received an offer to teach at a famous prep school, but they wanted someone who was married. I proposed to my girlfriend at the time, and she said yes. We lived at the school for a few years, but she got bored. I did too, so I ditched the job and somehow ditched her, too, in the process. There were no hard feelings. We're still friends to this day. She sends me pictures of her grandkids, and I send her pictures of the places I travel to. It's a good deal for both of us and makes us both happy."

"That's civilized. My ex has remarried, but he's still my best friend."

"How does his wife like that?"

"Not so much," Emma said, remembering Amber's poisonous looks. "But she's gotten used to it."

"Tell me about your marriage."

"Not much to tell. We got married in medical school, we had a girl, then he met someone younger and prettier. The oldest story in the world."

"Not for those who have to go through it."

Emma shrugs. "How about your third marriage?"

"I..."

Emma's pager goes off, her phone starts ringing, and the "Bright Star" announcement screams out of every speaker.

"What the heck is that?"

But Emma is halfway down the first set of stairs toward Medical because that's where the Bright Star was called for. That means somebody died in Medical, and Emma knows there was not a single patient there when she left. Nobody but the staff. Which of them is the Bright Star for?

CHAPTER 42

The steps to Medical are so crowded that Emma has to elbow her way in. The stretcher team blocking the door steps aside to let her through.

The waiting room is empty except for Sue, looking ashen, sitting between two children and holding their hands. The girl must be four, the boy a bit older. They're both dressed up, but their huge eyes are scared, and their pretty clothes are covered in blood.

Emma rushes to them, but Sue shakes her head.

"They're fine. Go to the ICU."

The body occupying the ICU stretcher is dressed up too. Her purple Indonesian dress is embroidered with gold, and her tiny feet in pretty sandals have carefully manicured red toenails. But the flowers in her jet-black hair are soaked in the blood spurting from the gash in her scalp, her eyes are closed, and her open mouth gasps for air.

Her hands shaking, Marico is working on an IV to her right. To her left, Fajar listens to her heart, his decomposed face covered in blood. Dana stands at the head of the bed, holding an oxygen mask over her face and squeezing the blue bag to pump air into her lungs.

"What happened?" Emma asks.

"She was walking on the deck, and an outboard engine fell on top of her," Dana answers.

"An engine?"

"Yes. From a crane."

Emma wonders what the crane was doing there and what the woman was doing under the crane. But there's no time for that right now. Now it's time to keep her alive if possible. The questions will come later.

"I have an 18 in the right AC," Marico says.

"Let's start fluids. Do we have blood on the ship?"

"No. But we can get blood from the sailors to transfuse her. We need to type and cross her first. The same with the sailors."

"Please do. And let's get some labs going. Type and cross, H and H, coags, lytes, the lot. How's her breathing?"

"Not hearing much. She's got decreased breath sounds bilaterally. I think she's got at least one pneumothorax. Maybe bilateral," Fajar answers.

"Heart?"

"Strong."

"Let's set up for bilateral chest tubes. Fajar, you take one side; I'll take the other. And we need more help here. Get somebody to take care of the kids so Sue can come to help us. Marico, get her on the monitors, please. Dana, I'll take the airway. Please obtain a second IV and start fluids. Fajar, I need a C-collar."

Emma palpates the woman's neck for a pulse. It's fast, as expected, as her heart struggles to keep up with the blood loss. She slides her fingers along the spine and slips the rigid collar around it to immobilize the neck. She palpates the face, looking for facial injuries, but she doesn't find any.

She pulls up the eyelids to check the pupils. They're equal and reactive, but the woman is deeply unconscious. She doesn't even move when Dana sticks a needle in her arm to get a second IV. She's breathing on her own, but she's struggling. Her oxygen saturation should be 100 percent, but it's only in the eighties, so Emma slips a nasal cannula under the mask, opening the oxygen tube as far as it goes.

"Get ready to intubate. Dana, you get the head. I need in-line stabilization to protect the spine."

"What do you want for intubation?" Sue asks.

"A hundred of fentanyl and 125 of Sux."

"Any versed? Or propofol?"

"No. They'll just drop her blood pressure. And she doesn't need them; she's out already. Just the fentanyl to dull the pain."

Emma grabs the #4 Miller, a lighted foot-long steel blade an inch wide, and scissors her fingers between the woman's teeth. With her left hand, she opens her mouth and slides in the blade, lifting the tongue. Her right hand pushes down the Adam's apple to expose the airway.

But something funny is going on inside the woman's throat. The glistening pink mucosa has a spongy texture like Emma has never seen before, and it bubbles around the laryngoscope like it's alive.

"What the heck?"

Her right hand feels the throat. It's spongy and swollen, and it crackles under her fingers. It's crepitus, Emma thinks. The broken ribs pierced the lungs, and the leaked air dissected through the tissues, swelling everything and narrowing the access to the airway. *It's awful already, and the*

*more I wait, the worse it will get. If I don't get the airway now,
she's dead. With all this swelling, I can't even get a
cricothyrotomy.*

Emma pushes the blade in and up, lifting the head off
the stretcher. Her arm shakes under the weight, but she
bites her lip and doesn't let go until she catches a glimpse of
white cartilage blinking from the foamy mass of pink tissue.

"Endotracheal tube."

Sue slaps the tapered plastic tube in her hand, and
Emma slides it along the blade, looking to get it over the
white spot marking the arytenoids that gate the tracheal
opening.

The pink tissues swell around the tube, blocking its
passage. Emma twists it to align the taper with the tracheal
opening and wiggles it to slide it in.

The tube gets stuck in the pink mess, but one more
wiggle and a push allow it to glide in. Hoping that she got it
home, Emma fills the balloon with air to secure it and
attaches the CO_2 detector to check its placement.

The CO_2 detector's purple fades to tan, indicating that
the tube is where it belongs, and Emma lets go of the breath
she didn't know she'd been holding. She attaches the ETT
tube to oxygen and watches the oxygen saturation waver for
a moment, then climb to the high eighties, then to the
nineties.

"Let's secure the tube and move on to the chest tubes."

Sue secures the tube with tape and ties it so it can't
dislodge as Emma listens to the lungs. They sound more
and more remote.

"Blood pressure's dropping," Dana says.

Of course. Now that they are pumping pressurized air
into the woman's damaged lungs, the air escapes into the

adjoining tissues and stops the blood from filling the heart. For this woman to live, they need to release the pressure and do it fast.

CHAPTER 43

Emma glances at Fajar who stands at the end of the bed.

"Let's get those chest tubes in before she codes. Marico, cut off her clothes."

They should have done that sooner, but this isn't Emma's ER, where the trauma team is a well-oiled machine seeing a dozen traumas a day, and the hospital sends in help as soon as they call a code. Here, it's just the five of them. No extra nurses, pharmacists, EMTs, CNAs, respiratory therapists, or X-ray techs. Not even the well-versed security people and knowledgeable clerks always ready to lend an extra hand.

Marico cuts the bloody purple cloth, exposing the golden skin underneath. The naked woman on the stretcher is almost as wide as she is long. The subcutaneous emphysema, the air that broke through her tissues and swelled her like a balloon, makes her look like the Michelin woman. Finding the bony landmarks in the traumatized, swollen body is next to impossible. Even the face looks humongous and scary.

Emma grabs a bottle of iodine and splashes it on the woman's side, near her breast. That's where the chest tube should go, she thinks. Anterior axillary line, fourth to fifth intercostal space. That's around the level of the nipple. She digs her index finger in, looking for the firmness of the ribs to find the dip between them, the space she's looking for. She pushes harder against the doughy consistency, but the muscles and ribs no longer feel like muscles and ribs. They feel like bubbling dough, and they crackle under her fingers.

"Blood pressure 75/30," Sue says.

She's running out of time. *It's now or never*, Emma thinks. She reminds herself of the one thing that gives her courage whenever she has to do a risky procedure that may kill her patient: I'm not killing this woman. I didn't bring her here, and I didn't drop that engine on her. With this risky procedure, I'm giving her a chance to live.

"Scalpel."

Somebody slaps a scalpel into her hand. Emma takes a deep breath and leans over the bloated body that no longer looks human. She stabs it with the scalpel, then lengthens the cut.

She'd typically need about a one-inch cut, but not today. The air leaked into the chest wall, making a deep dark hole between the skin and the place the tube must reach. There are inches of skin, fat, and lots of air before reaching the intercostal space to slip the tube inside the chest cavity that needs decompression.

Emma expands the cut. The wound bleeds and hisses, spitting out bloody air. Emma probes it with her left index and feels the firmness of the rib. She slides her finger above it to find the space she's looking for.

She stabs the pleura, the chest cavity lining, with her

finger. But the membrane is tough and elastic and won't break. It's like trying to pop a balloon with your finger. She'd do better with a trocar or a scalpel, but she's afraid she'd damage the lung even more.

"Blood pressure 68/30."

Emma swears between her teeth and pushes again, letting loose all her anger against the world's ugliness and misery. The membrane pops with a whoosh. A rush of hot air sprays blood on Emma's face as the chest cavity releases the pressure choking the heart.

One down, Emma thinks. She wipes the blood off her eyes on her arm and glances across to see how Fajar's tube is going. But Fajar isn't doing anything. He's just standing at the foot of the bed staring at Emma.

"Fajar? Can you place the other chest tube?"

Fajar shakes his head.

Emma sighs. It's not a straightforward procedure. Many doctors never learn to do it, but for a cruise ship doc with no backup, responsible for thousands of lives, that would come in handy. Oh well. Now that she's decompressed one lung, the other can wait for a moment.

"Come, I'll show you."

She moves to the woman's left side. She finds her spot, paints the area with iodine, then cuts into it with the scalpel.

"Then you stab it with your finger looking for the elastic membrane between the ribs, and you push through it to decompress. There, try it."

She reaches for Fajar's hand to show him, but he pulls back, his face white like he's about to faint.

What a squeamish doctor, Emma thinks. She shrugs and pushes her finger to rip the membrane. Another pop, another woosh, another spray of blood, and both sides of the chest are decompressed. Now all she has to do is to place the chest tubes and stitch them in to allow the lungs to re-expand.

"If I put in the chest tubes, can you secure them, Fajar? I'll show you how."

"I know how."

Emma slides in the thick chest tube, directing it up and anterior to reach the air outside the lung, then hands it to Fajar to secure. She moves back to the right side, slips the chest tube in and secures it, then grabs a stapler and staples the scalp wound to stop the bleeding.

She checks the vitals. Much better. "Blood?" she asks.

"We're still waiting for the type and cross."

Emma sighs. "Let's get her out of here. She'll be much better in a good ICU. They'll have everything she needs more than we do, and she's stable enough for transport. She won't get any better, but she'll likely get worse. Is there a family we can talk to?"

"Her children are in the waiting room," Sue says, and Emma remembers the two kids. They must have seen the horrific accident.

"Those poor kids! What a terrible thing to see! But where's their father? Who did she come here to see?"

"Me," Fajar says. "I'm her husband."

CHAPTER 44

E mma couldn't sleep that night, no matter how she tried. The memory of the poor woman's swollen body, the terrified kids' bloody faces, and Fajar's stricken expression haunted her whenever she tried to close her eyes.

She tried to tell herself that she'd managed to save the woman's life — maybe — but it didn't help. All she could think about was Fajar's face when she told him to put a chest tube in his wife and how she judged him when he couldn't.

Enough's enough. Emma glanced at the wine bottle she'd hidden in the back of her closet but decided against it. She was the only doctor on a ship with five thousand souls that was either cursed — and Emma didn't believe in curses — or had a homicidal maniac on the prowl. She needed her wits about her. A walk on the deck would have done her good, but outside access was restricted because of the high winds and rough seas. She cursed between her teeth, put on her sneakers, and headed to the gym to work out her frustration.

Too late for the passenger gym, she thought, so she tried to find the tiny crew gym Marico had shown her last week.

"It isn't much, but it's just for us. And it's open 24/7. Here, nobody wears fancy designer clothes or shows off. Well, the men sometimes do, but just to each other," Marico said.

She was right, Emma thought as she opened the door to a stark windowless room hidden in the ship's bowels. It wasn't much. Barely bigger than her cabin, it had just enough room for a treadmill, a bike, an elliptical, and a stack of free weights. And it was empty, but for a sweaty woman whose back muscles bulged under the weight of an overloaded barbell.

Wow. I wish I was half as good, Emma thought, grabbing a towel and heading toward the treadmill.

The barbell hit the ground with a clang.

"Hi, Emma."

"Dana? Wow! I didn't even recognize you! What an impressive physique you hide under those scrubs!"

Dana laughed.

"Thanks, I think. Working out keeps me sane. This is where I vent my frustration after dealing with Sue's antics the whole day and the demands of entitled patients every other night. Sometimes it feels like working out is the only thing in my life I can control. The rest of the time, I'm at everyone's beck and call."

"Isn't that the truth!" Emma said, fumbling to turn on the treadmill and failing.

"Let me help you. Whenever I try a new machine, I spend half of my time figuring out which button to push."

Dana pushed a few buttons and got the treadmill going.

"Thank you. Unless you want to use it?"

"No, thanks. I'm done with the weights, so I'll just jump

on the bike for a few minutes to keep you company. How are you doing?"

"Hanging in there. You?"

"Me too. Today was terrible, but it could have been worse. I'm telling myself that I'm better off than Fajar. I wouldn't like to be in his shoes."

"Neither would I. Poor man."

"What do you think is the chance she'll make it?"

Emma shook her head.

"I don't know. Not great."

"That's what I thought. It's terrible."

"You know, Dana, it's bad enough to lose your spouse, but after something like that? How do you even recover from it?"

Dana sighed.

"It takes time. Two years ago, when I lost my husband, I was devastated. I thought my life was over and I would never get over him. But days go by, then weeks and months and years, and slowly you start to live again and move on."

"I'm so sorry about your husband, Dana. I had no idea. What happened to him?"

"He had an accident."

"Car?"

"No. He was a mountaineer, and he loved to climb. Rock climbing, ice climbing — he did it all. We both did. But one day, when we were climbing Negoiu Peak, the second highest in Romania, he took a wrong step. He fell two hundred feet. It takes a long time to fall two hundred feet, you know. Almost four seconds. An eternity. I always wondered what he thought of as he fell."

"Were you there?"

"I was."

"That must have been terrible."

"It wasn't easy. But as I said, you get used to it. And, to tell the truth, as much as I loved him, he was just a cheating SOB. With everything I learned after he died, I didn't know whether to mourn the love of my life or to be glad I got rid of him."

Her eyes hard, Dana pushed on the pedals with renewed vigor.

"I'm so sorry," Emma said.

"Oh well. Life is what life is. And it was long ago. Not to mention that he got what he deserved. How about you, Emma? Have you ever been married?'

"Yep. Long ago."

"What happened?"

"Same old story. He found someone younger and prettier and left."

"You miss him?"

"Not anymore. But I stopped trusting men."

Dana laughed. "Good for you. You don't have to trust them to have fun."

Emma shrugged. "I don't..."

The door opened. A handsome man with dark eyes and a ponytail, dressed in tight shorts and a cutoff T-shirt stepped in.

"Hi, Dana."

"Hi, Antonio. How come you're here instead of the real gym? Trying to hide from your fans?"

Antonio shook his head and laughed.

"I got tired of being social, so I thought I'd go for a real workout." He turned to Emma.

"Hello."

"Emma, Antonio is the spa manager and the most coveted man on the ship. Antonio, this is Dr. Steele."

"Glad to meet you, doctor. I've heard a lot about you."

"About me?"

"Of course. Word travels fast here. A cruise ship is pretty much like a village; everybody knows everything about everyone."

"Not quite everything," Dana murmured.

Antonio gave her a sharp look. Dana stepped off her bike, wiped the handles, and headed to the door.

"I need to get going if I want to get any sleep. And I'd better. After a day like this, who knows what tomorrow will bring?"

"You're right. I'm coming," Emma said.

"Sweet dreams, ladies," Antonio said, lifting a couple of massive dumbbells like they were feathers.

"What a glorious specimen," Dana said as the door closed behind them. "Too bad he's taken."

"Is he married?"

Dana laughed.

"Antonio? Oh, no. He's not married. But he's got a very special friend."

Emma was still pondering Antonio's friend when she got to her cabin, but then she forgot.

Somebody had been through her stuff. Again.

CHAPTER 45

Dear Margret,
    I hope you are well. I miss you all very much, and I treasure every one of your emails and pictures. Please keep them coming.

I am doing well, and I'm getting used to life on the ship. The sea is beautiful, and the weather is perfect. It's in the seventies and sunny every day.

We are still in Indonesian waters. What a wonderful country! Did you know that it has more than seventeen thousand islands, including Bali, Borneo, and Papua New Guinea? Indonesia is the world's fourth most populous country and the most populous Muslim country. It has an extraordinary biodiversity, with unique endemic species from orangutans and Komodo dragons to birds of paradise. But the best things about Indonesia are its cuisine and its friendly people.

Our steward Mohamed, who takes care of Medical, taught me to make nasi goreng, Indonesian fried rice. That's the Indonesian national dish. The shrimp paste and the caramelized soy sauce make it spicier and more flavorful than the Chinese version. I also love rendang, a rich curry with slow-cooked meat in coconut milk flavored with pemasak, a spicy mixture of ginger, turmeric, lemongrass, chili, shallots, and garlic. I bought some to bring home, and I can't wait to cook it for you and share stories over good food and a decent Bordeaux.

I also got to meet a few people since half of our crew is Indonesian, including Fajar, the crew doctor, who is very charming. Yesterday in Semarang, I met his wife and lovely children when they came to visit him on the ship.

I have to commend the cruise company for welcoming the crew's families on the ship to let them see where their loved ones live and work when they're away from home. They even organized a tour of the crew areas and an ice cream bar in the crew mess. It was lovely to see the kids' joy.

Unfortunately, Fajar's wife had an emergency. She had to return ashore, so I didn't get to know her very well, but I hope I get a chance in the future. Fajar had to go with them, so I have both his patients and mine for now. That's good since it keeps me busy and out of trouble.

I made some other new friends. I already told you about Hanna. Thanks to her, I met Frank, a good-looking biologist who lectures on the boat. He also lectures me every time we meet. He's interesting and informative, though his style could use some improvement. I wonder if he's on the spectrum. He's brilliant and has a great sense of humor and a baffling disregard for the usual conventions that rule conversations. Being with him is half the time annoying and half the time refreshing, but always exciting and challenging.

I also met the captain's wife, a dazzling Thai lady named Nok, who used to be a bar girl. Bar girls are pretty young ladies who spend their time in bars, entertaining customers and encouraging alcohol consumption. I'm not sure if they also offer sex for money, but I wouldn't be too surprised.

Nok is funny, fascinating, and a most unlikely match for the captain, a stuffy Dutch at least twenty years older who doesn't know how to smile. I can't wait to know her better, which should happen soon since she invited me for a spa date tomorrow. We'll chat and get pampered.

My friend Sue struggles a little. She had a big fight with her husband Will, so he disembarked a few days ago, and she seems to miss him a lot.

My other new friend is Dana, the Romanian nurse. She's from Transylvania, which turns out to be a real place. She told me she grew up just a few miles away from Dracula's castle. She's a charming girl who always has something interesting to say.

Marico, the other nurse, is from the Philippines. She's lovely, and I like her a lot. She's good friends with Sue and helps her through this challenging time.

Our next stop is Kuala Lumpur, the capital of Malaysia. Its symbol, the Petronas Towers, used to be the tallest buildings in the world until not long ago. And everybody raves about their panang curries. But I'm unlikely to make it there since it's at least an hour's drive from the port, and I don't have that kind of time between my clinics.

After KL, we're off to Singapore, then to Bangkok. I hope to get off the ship in Singapore for a few hours, but it all depends on who's sick.

That's it for now since I have to prepare for my afternoon clinics. Give my best regards to Taylor and Hope. How are they doing? Also, to Victor, Amber, and their whole menagerie.

But my warmest hugs are for you and Guinness. Please buy her a big marrow bone for me, boil it with carrots, onions, and Montreal seasoning, and give it to her. I know it's not Vera's special rosemary garlic chicken cookies, but it's the best I can do. Please tell her that I love and miss her and will be back soon.

Love you and miss you,

Emma

CHAPTER 46

The morning clinic was light, since most passengers had left the ship early to drive to KL for the day. Emma didn't, but she didn't mind. She had a date with Nok for a spa day of pampering and relaxation.

She brushed her teeth twice to remove the coffee stains, gathered her hair on top of her head, and slipped on some Chocolate Dream lipstick. She knew she shouldn't since she would sweat it all out in the sauna, but she needed to feel better about herself. She couldn't compare to Nok, but she could at least look her best.

The pretty receptionist with a plumeria flower behind her ear greeted her with a blinding smile and handed her a glossy menu. Emma sunk into the comfortable armchair to browse the luxurious-sounding treatments at even more luxurious prices. Body nectar nourishing wrap. Intensely cleaning Dead Sea scrub. Intoxicating grape thirst quencher. Electrifying facial rejuvenator. Every one of the fifty-minute-long treatments cost hundreds of dollars more than Emma's full-day pay, some of them twice and three times more, and Emma started wondering if this was a good idea. The cruise company seemed to believe that working on a ship was a labor of love. She gets free room and board, so paying her a fair wage on top of that would be overkill.

When she left home, Emma was so intent on seeing the world that she didn't worry about working for pennies. But since nothing else here is free, from the wine and the internet to the shore excursions, the spa is a luxury she can ill afford.

"Hi, Emma. So good to see you."

Dressed in a low-cut summer dress with jungle prints in a rainbow of colors, Nok is a ray of sunshine. Her throaty voice sounds like she's smiling even when she's not, and Emma can't help but succumb to her charm.

"Good to see you, Nok."

"Have you been here before?"

"No."

"Well then, lucky me, I get to show you this lovely place. Have you figured out what you want?"

Emma glances back at the brochure and settles on the least expensive item on the list.

"An icy-hot pedicure, maybe?"

"What else?"

"I don't know. What will you have?"

"Oh, I'll have the Thai massage, of course. And maybe a relaxing facial?"

"Where's the Thai massage?"

"It's not on the list. The spa doesn't advertise it since it doesn't make much money. Most money comes from selling products — face creams, masks, and serums. The girls and the company earn commissions on everything they sell, so that's what they push. The Thai massage doesn't sell anything, so what's the point of advertising it?"

"What is a Thai massage?"

"You never had one?"

"No."

"Well, your day has come. I'll buy it for you. Khun Aoy here is fantastic. You'll thank me later."

"But..."

"No worries. It's cheap. And on shore day, treatments for the staff are half-price."

Nok chats to the pretty receptionist in a melodious language that Emma doesn't understand.

"We're all set. We'll enjoy the sauna and the Turkish baths, then we'll get our treatments. You get your pedicure as I get my massage, then we switch."

Emma sheds her dress, takes a shower, and joins Nok in the Finnish sauna. The light wood benches are almost too hot to touch, and the air smells like pine, reminding Emma of the Adirondacks. She slips in and slams the door behind her. On the highest shelf, Nok lies on her white towel. Her olive skin glows with sweat and her eyes are closed. But for the color, she looks like an antique marble sculpture, and Emma can't stop staring. She sits on the second bench, as far as she can, holding her white towel wrapped tightly around her and lets the heat seep into her bones.

"Take off your towel and lie down. You'll feel better and sweat better. That's what the sauna is about: getting rid of your toxins and worries."

Nok doesn't open her eyes, and Emma wonders how she knows. She unwraps the towel and lies on the bench, feeling the heat embrace her and letting her body open up to the cleansing steam.

"Isn't it better?"

"Yes, it is."

"Good. That's the whole point, isn't it? You shouldn't

deny your body, Emma. There's nothing shameful about it. That's where your soul lives. Give your soul a joyful home."

"I never thought about my body this way."

"How do you think about your body?"

"Like a tool. It's there to help me do what I need to do."

"That's a little simplistic, but even if it was so, you should still treat it right if you expect it to serve you. You wouldn't expect a knife to work without sharpening or a car without gas and oil. Even if you see it as a tool, you must care for it properly. But your body is much more than a tool. Your body is you. You should love it and be nice to it. You should feed it well, rest it when it needs it, and give it pleasure. Rejoicing is good for the body and for the soul."

Emma's heart beats faster. She doesn't know if it's the heat or Nok's soft voice.

"I know that's not the Western way. Many Westerners think pleasure is a sin and should therefore be punished. That's why so many are into S&M. They confuse pleasure and pain. Or at least they can't separate them. But that's not the Thai way. Have you ever heard about Sanuk?"

"No."

"It's a Thai word that means fun. We, Thai people, think everything should be Sanuk. Food. Ambiance. Conversations. Sex. Sanuk makes life more fun and makes us nicer people."

Emma remembers captain Van Huis's frowning face. She'd like to ask Nok about her husband's feelings about Sanuk, but she bites her tongue. That would be rude and unaccounted for, no matter how interesting.

She tries to soften her shoulders and relax, but the scorching heat makes her dizzy.

"Let's go chill and rest," Nok says. She holds the door for Emma, leaving her towel behind. Emma follows, wrapped in her sweaty towel. Nok laughs and dips in the cold blue pool meant for after-sauna chilling. Seconds later, she emerges shuddering and lays down on a marble bench facing the huge windows open to the immensity of the sea.

Emma plunges too, and the cold water freezes the breath in her chest. That's what we should do with the patients in SVT, supra-ventricular-tachycardia, she thinks. That water would fix them.

She wraps herself in a fresh towel and lies on the bench next to Nok's.

The shock of going from scorching heat to freezing water relaxes her body and softens her into a puddle. It's like a massive weight fell off her shoulders.

"Thanks for inviting me, Nok. This is the best time I've had in a while."

"I heard you've been busy. Will Fajar's wife make it?"

Who knows? The woman had extensive injuries. Multiple broken ribs, bilateral pneumothoraces, a significant head injury, and who knows what else? Paralysis from a broken neck is not out of the question.

"I hope so."

"Everyone talks about how you saved her life. They say she'd be dead if it wasn't for you."

"If it wasn't me, it would have been someone else. But I'm thrilled we were able to keep her alive."

"Of course you are. I'm not sure that everyone feels the same, though."

"What do you mean?"

"Well, whoever fooled around with that crane didn't count on you saving her. When they dropped the engine on her, they planned to kill her."

"What makes you think someone fooled around with that crane?"

"You don't know?"

"Know what?"

"Somebody moved that crane where it had no business being. Whoever that was, they dropped that outboard engine on the promenade deck from twenty feet high. That couldn't be an accident. It was a well-planned attack. They managed to get her without touching Fajar and the kids."

"How do you know?"

"I'm well-connected, remember? Ever since this happened, Pieter has done nothing but investigate how someone could get hold of that crane. He's sweating bullets to keep the Indonesian police from locking up the whole ship. I've never seen him more miserable, and I've seen him miserable enough. Those stupid people even tried to pin that murder on Fajar, who was walking with her on the deck. I guess they thought it easier to solve two crimes in one go."

"She's not a murder victim. Not yet."

"Good point. Hopefully, it won't get to that."

"What do you think? Who do you think did this?"

"One of his other women, I bet. He just can't keep his zipper closed. Fortunately, most don't take him seriously. He's a great one-night stand, but no more. But some become obsessed. They think he's the real deal, with forever on the menu, and they get mad when he moves on."

"You mean you... you..."

"Of course. Fajar wouldn't miss anyone with a skirt. Fortunately, we have no Scots. You didn't?"

"No."

"Why not?"

Emma shrugs.

"Neither of us was interested."

"Speak for yourself. He'd be interested in a goat if she was available."

Emma stops to ponder.

"But you're married to the captain."

"I couldn't help but notice. The captain was busy at the time."

"Aren't you afraid he'll find out?"

Nok laughed.

"He knows already. I told him. Pieter and I have an open marriage that suits us both. We can enjoy our... friendships as long as we're discreet. We both enjoy spending time with other people."

Emma tries to wrap her brain around the kind of marriage where you talk about your lover with your spouse, but she fails.

"Speaking of that. I'd love to spend more time with you, Emma. You are fascinating, and I hope we get to know each other better."

Her hand comes to rest on Emma's thigh, and Emma freezes. She doesn't know whether to run for the door or pretend she doesn't notice when the pretty receptionist opens the door.

"Your treatments are waiting. Would you like a drink?"

CHAPTER 47

Emma couldn't find sleep that night. She twisted and turned in her bed, thinking about what Nok had told her.

First, about the crane accident that apparently wasn't an accident. After the clinic, Emma walked up to the promenade deck to look at the crane. She found it but couldn't figure out how one could make it work. A metal ladder led to the crane's cabin ten feet above, and the door was locked. No way could anyone get there by mistake and push the wrong button. And operating that crane must require some specialized knowledge that not everybody has. Emma couldn't do it without instructions. But who could? Maybe the same person who killed Amanda? And pushed Gloria down the stairs?

Emma also wondered what had happened to Fajar. When his wife got rushed to the hospital, Fajar and the kids followed, accompanied by two policemen. He never returned, and Emma wonders if he's at the hospital or in jail. And what happened to the kids?

The other thing on her mind is Nok. Was that what she thought it was? Was Nok propositioning her? Or is it just the cultural difference?

Emma doesn't think so, but she's never been propositioned by a woman before, so she's not sure what to think. But, come to think of it, she doesn't really know what to think about being propositioned by men either. It doesn't happen that often.

Enough of this. Emma sits up. It's still dark, but since she can't sleep, she may as well go for a walk. One of the most magical things on the ship has been watching the sunrise and seeing dolphins once in a while. She slips out quietly and takes the stairs to the ninth deck, where she can see miles and miles of sea.

The sky starts fading in the east, and Singapore's skyline emerges from the darkness. A group of strange skyscrapers comes to life against the morning sky, and Emma takes picture after picture trying to capture the view.

"Ready for today's lecture?"

It's Frank, taking pictures with his massive camera. Emma smiles.

"Of course, professor."

"Good. I arranged for a car to pick us up at eleven, should you be able to escape."

"Maybe? But tell me about it."

"Singapore is an archipelago of sixty-three islands, and a quarter of its land is reclaimed from the sea. The city was founded by Sir Stamford Raffles in 1819 as a trading post of the British Empire. Now it's an independent country and Southeast Asia's largest port."

Slowing down to a crawl, the *Sea Horse* zigzags between the undulating shores of the many scattered green islands.

Ships of every size, shape, and color navigate the narrow canals, miraculously avoiding each other. Like a swarm of worker bees heavy with pollen, they're all loaded with piles of containers and fly their country's colorful flag.

"Singapore prides itself on its history, but it moved past it. It was part of Malaysia for a while, but then it declared its independence to become a purposefully multiethnic country. Most Singaporeans are Chinese, Malay, or Indian; they have four official languages, including English. Believe it or not, you're looking at the most expensive city in the world. It has more millionaires per capita than New York and more income inequality. But, thanks to the government that subsidizes education, healthcare, and childbearing, it has one of the highest standards of living in the world. Even the poor enjoy free healthcare, clean air and water, and one of the highest life expectancies."

The ship veers again, and they approach a group of five skyscrapers like Emma has never seen before. Tall and ghostlike, they rise from one of the green islands, seeming to lean toward each other. The triangular tops frame nothing but air, as if the vultures defleshed them, leaving behind nothing but the naked metal skeletons.

They're both hauntingly beautiful and scary. Seeing them shifts something inside Emma. She feels something will change her life forever, and she shivers.

Frank feels it.

"You OK?"

"The buildings..."

"The Reflections at Keppel Bay?"

"Those."

"Yes. They're condos. Interesting architecture, don't you think? They are just one example of the architectural wonders Singapore is proud of. If you get out, I'll show you more."

"Yes."

But Emma doesn't want to see more. She stares at the ghost buildings and wonders how they could be an omen just for her.

CHAPTER 48

Emma comes down to her clinic to find Sue at the medical desk. She nods and walks into her office without a word. They have long left any pretense of talking to each other unless it's essential for patient care. With Fajar gone, they've been too busy to worry about each other, which suits Emma perfectly.

She's finishing yesterday's notes when Sue walks in.

"Have you heard about Fajar?"

"No."

"He's... he's doing OK. They think his wife may make it after all."

"I hope so. That was a horrific accident."

"Yes. An accident. Just wanted to tell you that you did a good job saving her life."

Emma glances up, wondering what got into her.

"Thank you. I didn't do it. We all did. I couldn't have done it alone."

Sue smiles a narrow smile devoid of glee.

"Yes."

She disappears, and Emma wonders what that's all

about. Sue has never tried to be friendly, so this opening worries her. It's hard to believe that Sue suddenly overcame all her bile just because Emma managed to get in a chest tube.

But the patients start coming, and when the clinic is over, it's time to rush off the ship. Mr. Li and his Lexus are waiting.

Mr. Li bows deeply and opens the door. His narrow dark eyes and the thin beard with half a dozen hairs fluttering in the breeze make him look like the antique ink drawings of Chinese fishermen. Still, his English is perfect, and his driving superb.

The car glides on the wide, empty roads shaded by palm trees and glittering buildings. The sky is a dreamy blue, and the town, unlike any other metropolis, smells like the sea.

"Why are the roads so empty?"

"Here in Singapore, very few people own cars, miss. They are costly. To buy a car, you must get a COE, a certificate of entitlement that allows it to be on the roads for ten years. That COE alone is way more expensive than the car. After ten years, you need another COE, and that's rarely worth it. That keeps our roads empty and our air clean. That also subsidizes our MRT, Mass Rapid Transit. For a dollar, it whisks you from one end of town to the other."

"I'd sure like to have that at home," Frank says.

"Where's home?" Mr. Li asks.

"Los Angeles. When I still worked, my commute used to take two hours each way. It was almost like living in that car and breathing in the fumes. So did everyone else."

"Not here," Mr. Li says, parking the car.

"We are at Marina Bay, one of Singapore's most visited attractions. We'll walk through the Gardens by the Bay, cross over the Helix Bridge, then climb on top of the Marina Bay Sands to take in the best views in the city."

"What are the Gardens by the Bay?" Emma asks.

"They are the pride and joy of Singapore. Here, we don't have a lot of available land, so we make the most of the little we have. The Gardens are a set of ecological wonders meant to educate and entertain. The Flower Dome is the largest greenhouse in the world. It replicates a Mediterranean climate and features an always-changing display of flowers. The Cloud Forest is another greenhouse with a tropical mountain climate. The 138-foot Cloud Mountain is covered in orchids, ferns, and bromeliads and surrounded by a circular path with a hundred-foot waterfall that refreshes the air."

"What are those?" Emma asks, pointing to a forest of tall, tree-like things that don't look real.

"Those are the super-trees. They're vertical gardens that perform multiple functions. They grow unique ferns, vines, and orchids while mimicking the ecological function of real trees. They have photovoltaic cells to harness solar energy, similar to how trees photosynthesize. They collect the rain-water that we use for irrigation and fountain displays. They also serve as air intakes and exhausts for the greenhouses' cooling systems."

After wandering through the Gardens, Emma and Frank follow Mr. Li to the top of the Marina Bay Sands, the three skyscrapers holding an enormous surfboard-like platform that's the most photographed attraction of Singapore. The view from the top is almost as stupendous as the price of the entry ticket. From its top, you can see miles and miles of the sea and take in the architectural landscape.

"The two round buildings covered in spikes to your right are the Durian Buildings. They call them that because they resemble the world's most stinky fruit. The pedestrian bridge next to them was inspired by the DNA helix. It links Marina Bay Sands with the Formula One race circuit," Mr. Li says.

After taking hundreds of pictures, they return to the car. They're sweaty and tired, but Mr. Li isn't quite done with them.

"Singapore is a haven for car lovers. Once a year, we host the Formula One Singapore Grand Prix, which runs on the streets. But any day of the week, you can rent a Lamborghini Gallardo. For only $1100, you can take it anywhere in Singapore for four hours. If you have more time, for $2100, you can have a Ferrari F430 Spider for a whole day. If you're into classics, they have Rolls Royces and Bentleys."

Frank shrugs. "I'm more interested in lunch. How about you, Emma? Hungry?"

"Always hungry. But I'm afraid I'm running out of time."

"How about showing us the hawkers, Mr. Li?"

"What are the hawkers?" Emma asks.

"Food stands. You can have the most amazing Singaporean food for a dollar or two. Wanna try?"

"Sure."

"I'll take you to the best place," Mr. Li says. "Most hawkers these days are in what you'd call food courts in the basement of modern malls, but this place is different."

They drive through the narrow streets of China Town and stop by a large old building that's anything but elegant. The lower level turns out to be a crowded market that sells anything from electronics to socks, but Mr. Li takes them up the stairs to the second level. It's a vast open space the size of a barn with scattered melamine tables surrounded by long wooden benches. All around, food stalls offer Indian, Chinese, and Malay food.

Mr. Li points to the long row of stalls, each offering just one specific dish.

"With more than 260 food stalls, this is the largest hawker center in Singapore. You'll find anything your heart desires, from chili crab, Hokkien mee, barbecued stingray, frog porridge, prawn noodles, or pork intestines to carrot cake."

"I'm not sure about the frog porridge," Frank says.

"Would you rather have pork intestines?" Emma asks.

"We'll have chicken rice," Mr. Li says, joining the longest line.

Emma and Frank sit at a long table to watch the people. Old Chinese men leaning on canes, rubbing elbows with Indian high school girls and moms holding young babies, all staring in fascination at the food being prepared. Some stands are empty, some have lines that stretch beyond the corner, and nobody here looks like a tourist.

Mr. Li returns with the food, which doesn't look like much. Emma frowns at her plastic plate. It's a bed of white rice topped with a few slices of pale boiled chicken and three thin slices of cucumber served with a thimble of brown sauce and a cup of clear broth on the side. But the smell makes Emma's mouth water.

"It smells good."

Mr. Li smiles.

"Of course. Hainanese Chicken Rice is Singapore's national dish. Everyone has his own family recipe they keep secret. Still, they all have some combination of garlic, sesame oil, fresh ginger, green onions, shallots, and cilantro."

Emma takes a bite.

"This is unbelievable."

The succulent chicken melts in her mouth. The jasmine

rice is fragrant with ginger and shallots, and the thick brown sauce adds even more flavor. The clear hot broth gets drunk at the end to help digestion.

By the time she gets back to her cabin, she's exhausted but content. Singapore was a splendid day.

"You know, Emma, I'll miss you when I disembark in Bangkok," Frank said when he dropped her at the door of Medical.

"I'll miss you too."

"I actually mean it."

"Me too," Emma said.

He held her shoulders and looked into her eyes for an answer.

"Are you serious?"

"Of course."

"I could stay on. Not as a lecturer, but I could pay for the next leg of the cruise if you thought..."

Emma bit her tongue. Darn, she's clumsy.

"Frank, I like you a lot, but I'm a little burned out with men. I'm not looking for a relationship."

"I wasn't either. Then I found you."

"But I didn't find you. Sorry."

Frank left, his head hung low. Emma's eyes followed him. She felt like a jerk.

CHAPTER 49

That evening's clinic is a doozie. Singapore was the last stop before Bangkok, where most passengers will disembark. As they count the days and move from vacation mode to going home mode, depression sets in. And since most people can't tell depression from discomfort, they give in to the old aches and pains they forgot while they explored new places, basked in the sun, or raided the buffets. One after the other, they file into Medical, looking for a fix, reassurance, or at least a kind word.

When the last indigestion leaves, Marico slams the door shut. Emma drops onto a chair.

"That sucked."

Marico sighs.

"Big time."

"Are they always like this at the end of a cruise?"

"Always. They don't want it to end. Here on the ship, they get pampered day and night. From the captain to the stewards, we all do our best to please them, make them comfortable, and help them feel important. Once it's over, they go home where the weather sucks, there's nobody to do their dishes, and the kids only visit on Thanksgiving. They don't have much to look forward to."

"Oh boy, do I wish I could go home."

"Really? You don't like it here?"

"I do, sort of, but I miss my home, my family, and my dog. Most of all, I miss my freedom. I miss living on my own time instead of counting the hours between clinics and being tethered to the pager and the phone. Especially now that Fajar is gone and I have four clinics a day. I barely have time to brush my teeth."

"Does that mean you won't renew your contract?"

"I don't know what I'll do. I left my job and home, and there isn't much there to return to."

"No boyfriend?"

"I'm past that, Marico. I'm too tired and too old."

Marico laughs.

"How old are you?"

"Forty-two."

"That's not old."

"Old enough. I'm also past men. I just can't let them close. Even since I came on the ship, I had a chance at a relationship and blew it."

"Nice guy?"

"Sort of. Very smart, classy, and good-looking."

"And you said no?"

"I did."

"Aren't you sorry?"

"To be honest, I am."

"Maybe he'll come back."

"Maybe."

"What would you do?"

"I don't know. It depends on the day. I might just give it a try. You're right; I'm not that old yet."

Marico laughs. "Let's go. I'll buy you a drink."

The crew bar is the happiest place on the ship. Unlike the crew mess, where people rush in to grab a bite before returning to work, they come here to relax and connect. The TV plays some soap opera with the sound turned off. The beautiful girl sobs, brokenhearted when the sexy man abandons her, but no one cares. A handful of sailors, easy to recognize by their oily jumpsuits, drink whisky mixed with soda water and throw darts. Two officers in crisp white shirts sit at the bar, sipping on their beers and chatting with the bartender. But most of the low comfy armchairs are empty, so Emma takes a seat in the corner.

"What will you have?" Marico asks.

"A glass of wine."

"Red or white?"

"Red."

Emma watches the men throwing darts at the target on the far wall. The target seems safe, but they're having a blast, and Emma is glad she's not sitting any closer. Marico returns with the wine, red for Emma and white for herself. The girl on TV seems to have found a new suitor and is smiling again as they toast.

"Cheers. To new beginnings."

"To better luck next time."

The Chilean red is about as bad as Emma's ever had, but it's nice to chat with a friend who understands. Frank is fascinating, but he doesn't know what it's like to be a single woman and a mother stuck on a ship thousands of miles from home.

"How's your daughter?"

"She's doing well. She was first in her class in English, and my parents got her a kitten. She's overjoyed. There."

Marico shows her the picture of a glowing girl hugging a tiny tabby.

"I can't believe how much she looks like you. What happened to her father?"

Marico shrugs.

"We were sixteen. He was too young to get saddled with a wife and a kid. He's somewhere."

"Has there been anybody since?"

"A few failed attempts. But I'm a good Catholic girl, you know. We're supposed to save ourselves for marriage. But most men don't look for marriage. They just look for a good time."

It's late by the time Emma gets to her cabin. She brushes her teeth, takes a shower, then lies in bed to read a Bangkok guidebook. She may get out for a few hours with a bit of luck. She'd love to see the famous Wat Pho temple and get another Thai massage. That massage Nok booked for her was the closest thing to an orgasm she could think of that had nothing to do with sex.

Nok laughed when she told her.

"Of course. It gets you soft, mellow, and ready. For a little bonus, some massage parlors offer their customers a "happy ending."

"You mean... sex?"

"Of course not. Just a bit of extra massage to help with that joyous release."

Emma isn't sure whether that qualifies as sex or not, but it doesn't matter. She wouldn't know where to find something like that, even if she was interested. And she's not.

She puts away the guide and curls up to sleep when someone knocks at the door.

She checks the time. It's close to midnight. Who would

come to her cabin so late? If it was a medical emergency, they'd page her or call her, not knock at her door.

She stares at the door, wondering what to do. After all the things that happened, opening the door to someone she doesn't know sounds like a terrible idea.

They knock again, loud enough to wake up the whole darn Medical.

"Who is it?"

She can't understand what they say, so she cracks open the door.

CHAPTER 50

I t's Fajar. He looks thinner and older than when he left. Emma opens the door, and he slips in, closing the door carefully behind him.

"What are you doing here? I thought you were under arrest."

"I was."

"And?"

"They let me go."

"How come?"

"They got Amanda's autopsy results and found nothing pointing to me. They were even smart enough to figure that I couldn't have dropped that engine on my wife while I walked alongside her, holding the kids' hands. So they let me go."

"Impressive. How is your wife?"

"Much better. Anissa has seven broken ribs, a broken leg, and a concussion, but her spine's OK, and the brain looks alright. They lightened her anesthesia yesterday, and she woke up. It will take a long time, but she will hopefully recover completely."

"I'm delighted."

"Thank you, Emma. Thank you for saving her. She wouldn't have made it if it wasn't for you."

"Poppycock. If it wasn't me, it would have been someone else. I just did my job."

"I know. And I'm very grateful. If I live to be a hundred, I will never forget the look you gave me when I failed to put in that chest tube."

"I'm sorry. I didn't know she was your wife."

"I know. But I should have done it anyhow. Those few seconds could have meant the difference between life and death. But I couldn't. I couldn't bring myself to stab her with the scalpel and cut her to put the chest tube in."

"I don't blame you. I don't know that I could have done it to somebody I love."

"Oh, you would. For a woman, you're tough."

"Thanks, I think. But why are you back?"

"I have a job and a contract to complete. If I don't work, I won't get paid, and we need the money now more than ever."

"But who's going to look after the kids? And your wife?"

"My mother took the kids, and Anissa's mother will stay with her in the hospital. They will all be well cared for."

He looks at his hands that tighten into fists.

"And I'm back to find out who did this to her. And killed Amanda. I'll strangle them with my bare hands."

"What did you find about Amanda?"

"They didn't want to tell me at first, but they relented when I explained that I was her fiancé. They found no injuries, as we expected. It was most likely the insulin or some other hypoglycemic agent. Except..."

"Except for what?"

"She did have alcohol in her system — not much; she

must have had a couple of glasses of wine. But she was positive for opiates."

"Opiates?"

"Yes."

"Was she using?"

"Never."

"Then..."

"I think someone slipped something in her food or drink. She fell asleep, so they could inject her with all the insulin they wanted. She never woke up again."

"Who do you think would do this?"

"I don't know."

"You must have some idea."

"I don't."

Emma looks at him quizzically, and he shrugs.

"I really don't, whether you believe it or not."

"Could it be one of your ladies?"

"It sure could. But which?"

"How many do you have, for God's sake?"

Fajar blushes.

"Emma, I'm not proud of this. Not anymore. As a man, I used to think that it was my right and my duty to make women feel wanted and show them a good time. It was like a game I played with my friends, seeing who could score more ladies. It was fun. But after what happened to the women that mattered most to me, I'm no longer proud; I'm ashamed. Unfortunately, that won't bring Amanda back, nor will it make Anissa's recovery easier."

"How many?"

"A couple dozen or so."

"A couple dozen? On this ship alone? I didn't know we had that many women working on the ship altogether."

"Well, some of them weren't working."

"Passengers too? Really?" Emma shakes her head. "This is insane."

"Whoever did this is insane."

"That's one thing. Jealous too. And has some medical knowledge."

"Not necessarily. Everybody knows opiates would put you to sleep, and insulin can kill you."

"Maybe. But not everybody has it handy, plus a key to get to your cabin."

"They didn't have to have it. They may have used Amanda's own insulin, and she may have invited them to her cabin herself. Or at least opened the door."

"That's a point. What did Amanda do that evening?"

"I don't know."

"Well, find out then."

"How?"

"The steward may know. And the people she worked with: the performers. Or her parents."

"Good point. I'll do my best to find out. Anyhow, I just wanted to thank you for everything you did for my wife and me."

"Don't..."

Suddenly, Emma's pager goes off, and so does her phone. She's due to a medical emergency.

"Please go. I have to get dressed and go."

Fajar nods, and Emma opens the door. She looks left and right, making sure nobody sees him leaving her cabin at midnight. She waves him out just as Dana's door opens.

Dana looks them up and down. She smiles at Fajar's crumpled clothes and Emma's T-shirt that barely covers her bottom.

"Having fun, kids? Go get dressed before Sue sees you. She won't be happy."

Emma slams the door, wishing she'd never opened it. The last thing she needs is one of Sue's funks.

CHAPTER 51

The old man looks dead. But he's not. Yet.

His sweaty brow and gnarled old hands clutching his throat tell Emma everything she needs to know. She's rarely seen a more classic presentation of a heart attack, she thinks, as she places the electrodes for the EKG, Dana puts him on the monitor, and Sue works on an IV.

"What happened to you, sir?"

The man's words are labored.

"I woke up with this pressure in my chest and trouble breathing. It's just like my last heart attack."

"It figures," Emma mumbles, pushing the button to get the EKG. The machine whizzes and spits out a long strip of pink grid paper streaked with black zigzags that wouldn't mean much to most people. But to Emma and any medical person above a first-year medical student, it's clear as day. The EKG patterns have bloated into what medical people call "tombstones," the harbingers of a terrible heart attack.

"I'm afraid it's your heart again, sir. But we'll do our best to care for you."

Emma turns to Sue, who's getting blood.

"Let's get the TPA ready."

"Dana?"

Dana goes to get it as Sue puts the blood vials in the centrifuge and pushes the button to spin them. Emma turns to the patient.

"You have a blood clot that prevents the oxygenated blood from supplying your heart. We'll give you a medication called TPA. Many call it a clot buster. That will hopefully dissolve the clot and restore the blood flow to the heart. Are you on blood thinners?"

"Yes."

"Which?"

"I don't know. My wife has my medication list."

Emma sighs and sends a steward to get the list, but that's not good news. Blood thinners increase the risk of bleeding. But she has no choice. It will be days before they can get him into a hospital for catheterization, and by that time, much of his heart will be dead. Quite possibly him too. Time is heart muscle, so Emma must do whatever she can to help him now.

"There's the TPA."

Emma loads the syringe, hoping she's doing the right thing. She's never done this before since even her small community hospital has cardiologists on call, always ready to do a cardiac catheterization when the patients need it. Not here.

Emma takes a deep breath and attaches the syringe to the IV tubing.

"Ready?"

The man nods. His brow shines with sweat, and his face is scrunched in pain.

Emma pushes the medication in.

Now all they can do is wait. It will either work, which should improve his symptoms and his EKG, or it won't.

Emma sits by the stretcher watching the monitor when the steward returns pushing a wheelchair with a white-haired woman. Her eyes swim in tears as she hands Emma a medication list with a shaky hand.

"How is he doing?"

"Come and see for yourself."

The wheelchair gets pushed to the stretcher. They look into each other's eyes and hold hands.

"Don't worry, sweetheart, I'll be all right. Won't I, doctor?" the man says.

"If I have any say in it, you will," Emma says.

The woman cries quietly. The man touches her face.

"But if I don't make it... Tell Joe how much I loved him. I wasn't the most patient father, and I wish I had told him how much he means to me."

The woman leans over to lay her cheek on his hand. He caresses her hair.

Emma's heart tightens. She's half in awe and half heart-broken seeing these old people in love.

The man catches her eye.

"We've been married for forty-nine years. This cruise was a present from our son for our fiftieth anniversary."

"Is a present," Emma says, just as the monitor snaps into a new heart rhythm. It's abnormal as hell, but Emma recognizes it from her long-ago cardiology rotation. That's a reperfusion rhythm, and it's a sign the blood has come back to feed the heart.

"How are you feeling?"

"Better, I think." His pained expression is gone, and his ashen gray skin is gaining some color.

His wife sobs, and he touches her cheek.

"I'm feeling better, honey. Maybe we'll get to that fiftieth anniversary after all."

"Good work, doctor," Sue says.

Emma can't tell if she's serious or sarcastic. Nor does she care.

"Thanks, Sue. But it wasn't me. It was all of us."

Dana smiles.

"Isn't that the truth."

"Can I go back to my cabin?" the man asks.

"I'm afraid not. We need to monitor you and repeat your blood tests. We'll see how you look in the morning."

The steward takes the woman to her cabin, and Sue disappears as Emma and Dana tuck the man in for the night.

"I don't even know if it's late or early," Dana says.

"Both. Why don't you catch a couple hours of sleep as I watch him, and then we'll switch," Emma says.

"Are you sure?"

"Yep."

"Thanks."

Dana yawns and leaves. Emma sits on one of the metal chairs by the bed and puts her feet up on another to watch the monitor. His heart rhythm is back to normal, and the man has fallen asleep. The monitor beeps softly with his heartbeat. It's quiet in Medical.

Emma thinks about home. It's the afternoon now in New York, and Taylor must be in class. Unless she took Hope and Guinness out for a walk. It's winter there, so the paths must be covered in snow. Hope would smile her little alien smile, and Guinness would roll in the snow like a puppy. She's a winter dog, Guinness, and loves the first snow like kids do.

Emma feels tears run down her cheeks. She wishes she was there, throwing snowballs at Guinness. She'd leap and catch them, then break them in her strong jaws and spit them out, ready for the next.

CHAPTER 52

Emma shakes her head, trying to understand what's going on. Her stiff neck hurts after resting on the back of the chair, she's not in her cabin, and someone is shaking her.

"Come, quickly. His wife is dying," Marico says.

Emma remembers the white-haired woman.

"Where?"

"Upstairs. She fell from her wheelchair."

"How about him?"

"I called Dana. She's coming."

Emma grabs her doctor's bag and follows Marico up the back metal stairs, down a narrow corridor, down another set of stairs, then along another long corridor to a metal door opening into a dark room.

"In here."

Emma steps in. The room is dark but massive, and the meager light from the doorway falls over a toolbox and a coil of rope. This is like no cabin she's ever seen.

"Where are we?" she asks.

"Just where we should be."

The blow comes from behind. It's like a brick wall falling over her head.

The cartoon people were right. You do see stars, Emma thinks, then she thinks no more.

CHAPTER 53

Emma wakes up hurting. Everything hurts, from her left hip to the shoulder she's lying on and the hands behind her back. But nothing compares to the pain in her head. Emma has had migraines for twenty years but has never had one like this. The pain squeezes her brain into a blob of murky molasses. Every heartbeat pounds the blood in her head like a piston, so bad it makes her sick.

The darkness is so deep that Emma wonders if she's blind. This must be a nightmare, she thinks, and she struggles to sit up. A glimmer of light blinks behind her. It's her smart watch.

She tries to read it but can't bring her hands in front. Her wrists are tied behind her back. She pushes herself up on her elbow, trying to kneel, but her ankles are tied too. It takes her forever to get herself sitting. Her mouth is so dry she can't swallow, and she realizes she's gagged.

The floor is cold. She touches it with the tips of her fingers. It's metal, rough, and painted with paint that flakes off. She listens hard. Just the steady hum of the engines, much louder here than inside her cabin.

She tries to crawl on her knees to check the space, but it's pitch dark, and there's not much exploring she can do with her hands tied behind her back. She pulls, trying to release them, but whoever did this did it right. The ties won't give, but her wrists might.

Emma sits back down, trying to think, but she's so frozen she can't. How can it be so cold in the tropics? She smells for snow, but there's nothing but a whiff of engine oil and fumes.

This nightmare is nothing like her usual one. It feels so real that Emma wonders if it's a nightmare after all. But what else can it be? It's a bit much for a prank.

She takes a deep breath, then another, to steady her heart, and she digs into her memory for what happened.

The old man. He had a heart attack. She stayed to watch him, but she must have fallen asleep. Then somebody…

Marico. It was her all along. Lovely, sweet Marico. Telling her about her loneliness and showing her the picture of her daughter with her kitten. Buying her wine. Advising and helping her out. Lying to her. Trapping her.

And to think she always suspected Sue. Even Dana.

"I'm a good Catholic girl," she said.

Emma doesn't know much about Catholicism, but it's hard to believe that killing and kidnapping are what they preach. Though if you think back to the inquisition…

But why kidnap her? Why not just kill her, like she did with Amanda? And like she tried to do with Fajar's wife? It would have been easy. She was asleep and defenseless. She could have done it a dozen ways. Poison her, cut her throat with a scalpel, bludgeon her to death. Why go through the trouble to bring her here? Emma doesn't know, but she's pretty sure she won't like the answer. She'd better find a way to escape. But how?

She shrugs, and her shoulders hurt. She tries to readjust her arms, wishing she was one of those contortionists who can squeeze their bodies through their interlocked arms. But she's not. The day she can touch the floor without bending her knees will be a good day.

What would Houdini do? She's not Houdini, but could she maybe get some ideas?

Nothing comes to mind.

If at least she could undo the ties around her wrists. They're so tight they cut the blood supply to her hands, which are numb with cold. She fumbles in the dark, looking for something to cut them with. She kneel-walks until she bangs her head against something, throwing her migraine into an upward spiral. She stops to breathe, waiting for her nausea to abate.

She turns her back to the obstacle and runs her hands up and down it. It's a vertical ridge on the wall where the metal plates come together with screws. It's no sharper than a wooden spoon, but it's the best she's got, so she turns her back to it and slips it between her tied hands. She moves her hands up and down, up and down, again and again, trying to cut off her ties.

But nothing happens other than her shoulders killing her. It's an awkward position and hopeless work, but she keeps to it, biting hard on the gag in her mouth until she can't feel her hands.

Time for a break. She lies on her side to rest her back and thinks about Guinness. Oh, how she wishes her dog was here. Her heart full of longing, she tells her how she loves her, misses her, and wishes she could hug her hairy neck. She'd love to see her again, at least once.

The metal floor vibrates with the noise of steps, bringing her back to the here and now. Somebody's coming. Emma struggles back to her knees as she hears the door open. A blinding light hits her eyes and sends a tsunami of pain through her brain. Emma closes her eyes and turns away.

"How are you?"

After the profound darkness, Emma's eyes have trouble adjusting to the light. She glances at Marico but sees nothing but a dark shape behind the flashlight. She turns away again, taking in the room. It's a storage room, triangular and sparse, with a metal shelf a foot high all around it and boxes, tools, and coiled ropes on the floor. She finally knows where she is: This is that hidden place at the ship's bow where Marico brought her to the first night's crew party.

Marico laughs. "You can't talk. Good. It was high time."

On her knees in front of Marico, Emma looks down and scans the room for anything she could use. There isn't much. An empty beer can, a lighter, and a screwdriver under the long metal shelf, half-covered by a soiled uniform. A few large metal boxes. Hooks attached to ropes and some strange tools she doesn't recognize. A fire extinguisher.

"I'm here to make you an offer you can't refuse."

CHAPTER 54

Emma keeps scanning the room. There's a lantern hanging from the lower end of the ceiling. It's too high to reach with her hands tied, but if she got them untied...

And by the door, half-hidden under the long shelf, is her doctor's bag, the one she never goes anywhere without. That's where she dropped it when Marico clocked her.

She mustn't look at the bag.

"Are you listening?"

Emma nods.

"I need you to write a suicide note explaining how and why you killed Amanda and how you almost killed Annisa."

Emma stares at the door behind Marico. Thick metal, opening inward. She could conceivably block it with one of the metal toolboxes and make it impossible to open and shelter herself in here. Sooner or later, someone will come to look for her.

"Will you do it?"

Emma wonders if she could push the box to the door with her hands tied if she put her back into it. Depends on how heavy it is. But the heavier it is, the better it will hold the door closed.

"Will you do it?"

Marico's voice went up a notch. She's growing impatient.

Emma ignores her. It's not easy, as she kneels, tied and gagged in front of her, but there isn't much else she can do now. But plan.

Marico laughs. She steps forward and sits on a toolbox.

"Listen, Emma, you'll die anyhow. There's no way I can let you live after this, and you have no escape. Nobody will find you here for weeks. You'll die of thirst in a couple of days, rotting in your own piss since you can't even take off your pants. You'll suffer. You'll be cold, thirsty, and hungry and die anyhow. An awful, miserable slow death. But I can give you a lovely, sweet death. One good shot of fentanyl, and you'll die happy. You'll fall asleep and wake up in heaven. Or wherever you deserve to end up. I'm offering you a great deal."

Emma ignores her. That's the one thing she can do to hurt her. Marico needs to talk, and the more Emma ignores her, the angrier she gets. And angry people make mistakes.

"You will confess that you killed Amanda because you were jealous of her relationship with Fajar. You fell for Fajar the moment you met him. You thought he felt the same about you and would leave his wife to marry you. But he told you he loved Amanda, and that drove you insane. You begged and pleaded and humiliated yourself to change his mind, but he said no. So you decided to kill her."

Emma gives her a quizzical look.

"How, you ask? Easy. You slipped some opiates in her drink that evening. Then, when you knew she'd be asleep, you slipped into her cabin with your universal key and gave her a massive shot of insulin IV, so it works faster."

Marico's eyes look somewhere in the past as she keeps talking.

"After taking care of Amanda, you thought Fajar would return. But he didn't. He still didn't want you, even though he told you that he loved you and had never met someone like you. He had lied.

"He avoided you to chase others. The new singer. The yoga instructor. The captain's wife. Anyone but you. You saw him with the other women like he belonged to them, not to you, which drove you crazy. So, when his wife came on the ship, and he acted like a loving husband, you decided to show him. You had it all planned. You'd already stolen the key to the crane, so climbing up there and waiting for Fajar's wife to walk to Medical was a piece of cake. You waited for Fajar and the kids to pass, then dropped the engine."

Emma shakes her head.

"What do you mean no?"

Emma shakes her head again.

Marico looks at her, then at the door. She shrugs and leans over to take off her gag.

"Listen, Emma, nobody will hear you if you scream. Nobody but me, and I'd love it. But then I'll put the gag back. What do you mean no?"

Emma opens her mouth to speak, but she's so parched nothing comes out. She tries again, and her voice comes out so hoarse she can't recognize it.

"I was up on the deck with a friend. He knows I didn't do it. I was nowhere near that crane, and I couldn't be. This will blow up your suicide note."

"Which friend?"

"Which friend? So you can kill him too? Come on, Marico, you're getting silly."

"Silly? Me, silly?"

Marico's face turns purple, and her hands tighten into fists. Her lovely face scrunches into the ugly mask of hate, and Emma knows she's dying to hurt her.

"I am not silly. I am, in fact, brilliant. I was the only one who got the best of Nadja, Amanda, his wife, the little singer, and even you. Look at yourself. You're a pathetic loser. If you were smart, you'd have known long ago to leave my man alone. But no. You had to throw yourself at him. And just because you're American, he took you, as old and ugly as you are. But it's over. I've got you now. I will tell you what to do, and you will do it. If not today, tomorrow, or the day after. You'll do it when you've suffered enough. I can't wait to see you squirm. I tried to be nice to you, but you must make it difficult."

"Who's Nadja?" Emma asks.

Marico shakes her head.

"Another stupid woman who thought she could take my Fajar. She was wrong, of course. I bet he doesn't even remember her name, silly bitch."

Emma remembers Fajar's words. It feels like a lifetime, but it was only a few weeks ago, the day she embarked. "She was the third nurse and a lovely girl," Fajar had said. "She overdosed. Ever since that, we have had two people work together every time we access the controlled substances."

"You're wrong. He remembers her. How did you get her to overdose?"

Marico shrugs.

"I doctored her drink, then gave her a good dose of fentanyl. Like I'll do with you after you write that note."

Emma wonders why Marico doesn't type the note she wants on her phone as she did with Amanda. She doesn't know the password, but she can touch it with her dead finger to unlock it.

"You wonder why I won't write the note on your phone. I will if I must. But a handwritten note would carry more weight. Seeing how you type, nobody will believe you'd type your suicide note on your phone."

"What will you do with the body?"

"I'll leave it here. When anyone finds it, there won't be much to find."

"That would blow your suicide theory. Who'd believe I locked myself in this hole to starve myself?"

Marico sighed. "You have a point. I guess I'll have to throw you overboard. That's a problem since you're so fat, I can't carry you up the stairs. I'll have to quarter you and carry up the pieces."

A violent wave of nausea hits Emma. She bends over and vomits. Sour acid burns her throat, and the smell makes her retch again. She tries to wipe her mouth against her shoulder but she can't with her hands tied behind her back. She spits instead.

"I'll let you think about it. There's no point in suffering, Emma. It won't do you any good."

She stands up, heads to the door, and then turns once more.

"You know, I don't know what Fajar saw in you, but then he's not that choosy. Anything with a skirt will do. But I have to kill you, even though I know he'll drop you like he does all the others. You want to know why?"

"Why?"

"Because you, like a stupid bitch, saved his wife. Without you, he'd be free to marry me. I know I'm the one he loves. He just needs to understand it too."

"How about Amanda? He was going to marry her even though he had a wife."

Marico glares at her with disgust.

"I'm a Catholic. My religion would never allow me to do that."

Emma's jaw falls.

"How about everything else you've done?"

Marico slams the door, and the room sinks back into darkness.

CHAPTER 55

Marico's steps fade away. The silence and the darkness envelop Emma like a shroud.

Can't be much darker in a coffin, Emma thinks, waiting for her eyes to adjust to the darkness. But there's no adjusting. The darkness is too deep.

I need to untie my hands.

Emma goes back to sawing her ties against the metal seam. She does it over and over until her shoulders are about to fall off, but the rope holds.

How about the feet?

She lays on the cold metal floor on top of her achy hands and tries to saw the ties off her feet. She pushes until her hands go numb, and her back pain becomes unbearable. She's thirsty, achy, and exhausted, but she makes no progress.

Now what?

The black bag.

She crawls until she finds it. She lies on the ground and rests her face on the grainy leather. This bag was Victor's present the day she finished med school; since then, she has never left it behind.

Its metal clasp has a tiny lock, but thank God, she never locks it. She puts her teeth around the clasp and pulls. The bag clicks open.

Emma sits with her back to it and fumbles to get her hands inside. Her fingers rummage through her stuff until they find the long, sleek shape of the scalpel and close around it.

She opens it with her thumb and starts sawing the rope tying her ankles. Seconds later, her ankles are free.

She squeezes the open scalpel's handle in the heel of her left sneaker, then leans over and saws the rope tying her wrists against the blade. Three moves, and it's done. Thank God for scalpels, she thinks, closing it carefully and putting it in the side pocket of her scrubs.

She rubs her wrists and ankles to bring some blood back to her frozen limbs, then picks up her bag to look inside. She doesn't need light to do that like she doesn't need light to eat or brush her teeth. She's done it so many times that her fingers recognize every item.

Tourniquet. Gloves. Scissors. Gauze. A bottle of alcohol. Skin glue. And a penlight.

She turns on the slim penlight she uses to check the patients' pupils. The needle of light is barely strong enough to inventory the bag, let alone explore the room, but it's more than nothing.

She tries the metal door. It's locked, of course. And so heavy that she'd struggle to open it. Breaking it is out of the question.

Now what?

The pain in her wrists and ankles has faded somewhat,

but the thirst drives her nuts. She'd give anything for a drink. That's why blocking the door is a no-go. Locking herself in would mean a terrible death, just like Marico said.

How about making noise? Someone might hear it and come to check.

But that someone might be Marico, coming to kill her. And Emma's not ready. She's not prepared to die, but more importantly, she's not yet ready to fight.

She checks the fire extinguisher. It's one of the carbon dioxide fire extinguishers for Class B-C fires, like flammable liquids and electric fires. In orientation, they taught her how to use it. She didn't expect to ever need it, but it may come in handy. She pulls it out of its bracket and shines her tiny light to figure out how to unlock it, then lays it by the door, ready to use.

What else?

The lantern. She turns it on and then opens all the tool-boxes one after the other, looking for something she could use. Not much. A heavy wrench. Rope. A drill.

She makes a note of everything, then tidies up, hiding the wrench under the bench. When Marico comes, she shouldn't see anything changed. Otherwise, she'll get spooked and run away, locking her back in. She needs her to get close before the psychopath notices anything amiss.

Emma slips the tourniquet into her pocket with the scalpel, then ties the rope around her ankles, loose enough to let her pull out her feet. She turns off the light, wraps the other tie around her hands, then waits.

How long will it be? Who knows?

They must be looking for her by now. She glances at her watch, but the battery's dead. She must have been here for hours. Days, her parched throat screams, but she knows that can't be true. But she must have missed her morning clinic. They must have called her and paged her. When she didn't answer, they went to check her cabin, then started looking for her all over the ship. With a bit of luck, they'll come soon.

She waits. And waits.

She thinks about home. She thinks about her long walks with Guinness and playing with Hope, whose little triangular face makes her look like a pink alien. She wonders how Taylor handles the grown-up world. She always wanted to be a grown-up, Taylor. She wanted to tell the whole world to go funk itself. First of all, to Emma, who tried to keep her safe and teach her about responsibility. Taylor wanted freedom, but she wanted no responsibility, so Emma had to pick up after her again and again, until she left.

But there was more to Emma's leaving than Taylor. Some would call it her midlife crisis. And they may be right.

When her friend Vera died, after a well-lived life doing whatever she wanted, Emma realized that she had never done what she wanted. One way or another, she had always done what she had to. She did her job. She tried to be kind. She struggled to be a good doctor, a decent wife, and a good mother, but somehow, she failed at everything. So she watched life pass her by. She got older and older without love, the joy of motherhood, or having fun. She lived alone with only her wine to numb her pain and soften her sorrow. Then she'd had enough.

She quit everything to see the world and live the life she never had. But instead of that, she got herself trapped in this darn metal cage. And somewhere out there, there's the serial killer who locked her in here, and plans to kill her.

Emma is determined to fight her for her life, even though that raging lunatic is younger, fitter, and better prepared than a concussed, out-of-shape, middle-aged doctor with a flimsy scalpel and a fire extinguisher she's not even sure she can open.

She waits and waits. Her throat is dry, her eyes burn, and the cold seeps into her bones, robbing her of the little strength she has left.

CHAPTER 56

The bright light burns her eyes. Emma turns away, trying to ignore the pain in her hip and shoulder, frozen and numb from laying on them forever.

"Have you changed your mind yet?"

Marico shines her flashlight in Emma's eyes. She takes a water bottle from her shoulder bag and dangles it in front of Emma.

"You want water?"

Emma can't talk, so she nods. Marico laughs.

"Will you write the note?"

Emma shakes her head no.

"Well then..."

Marico heads to the door.

Emma sobs, and Marico stops.

"Are you sure?"

Emma shakes her head no.

"I hoped you'd be smarter than that. There, now."

Marico opens the bottle and pours cold water over Emma's face. Emma opens her mouth to drink, but Marico pulls back the bottle.

"Not so fast, my friend."

She puts the water bottle and the bag on top of the large toolbox by the door. She reaches into the bag and takes out Emma's planner, her pen, and a length of rope.

"We have work to do first. Come here."

Pretending that her ankles are tied together and keeping her hands behind her back, Emma knee-walks to the toolbox.

"I'll tie your left hand to the toolbox, then untie your right so you can write. Don't try anything funny, or you'll be sorry."

She leans over to tie Emma's hand.

Emma's right fist explodes into her face with a satisfying crack. That's got to be the nose, Emma thinks, as Marico drops the flashlight to the ground, leaving them in darkness. Emma grabs Marico's scrubs and pulls her to the floor, but Marico lands on top of her, and her hands close around her neck like steel talons.

"You bitch. I knew I couldn't trust you," Marico mumbles. Her fingers tighten, crushing Emma's throat and cutting the blood supply to her brain.

Emma's fingers struggle to unlock the claws choking her, but her hands, numb with cold, aren't strong enough. She hears panting, and realizes that it's her, struggling to breathe. She tries to stand, but Marico puts all her weight on her throat. Emma resists until she can't anymore, and she falls back banging her head against the hard floor.

Marico pulls her up. She knocks her down, then pulls her up again, slamming her head against the metal.

Thirsty for air, Emma manages to unclasp the iron hands choking her. She pumps her fist into Marico's stomach, and Marico groans. She puts her knees on Emma's chest and presses her to the floor, squeezing the last breath out of her. Emma struggles to push away the knees crushing her, but she can't.

Those merciless hands tighten around her throat again, and Emma's brain gets fuzzy. She reaches for the scalpel in the cargo pocket of her scrubs and opens it with her thumb. The scalpel is sharp but short and fragile. That inch-long blade won't do much damage unless Emma hits a vital organ, like Marico's face or her throat, but all she can see is darkness.

Emma lifts the scalpel and stabs into the darkness choking her. The claws let go of her throat, and a bloodcurdling scream tells her she didn't miss. She stabs again and again as a rain of hot, sticky blood covers her. Slick with blood, the scalpel slips out of her hand somewhere in the dark.

The killer's hands are gone. So is the knee crushing her chest. Marico let her go, but she's got to be here, somewhere. But all Emma can see is the darkness.

She holds her breath to listen, but other than the incessant engine hum there's nothing but her own heart pounding. She breathes softly and crawls toward where the door should be. The one thing Emma can't do is let Marico go. If she gets out, she won't return before she's sure Emma's dead, so she'll die here alone.

Metal clangs against metal somewhere to Emma's left. Emma reaches for Marico, grabs her scrubs and pulls her closer, but a horrible pain crushes her shoulder. Emma's collarbone cracks. Somebody screams, and it turns out it's her. Her useless left arm falls to the side like dead weight.

Emma bites her lips and reaches under the bench, where she hid the heavy wrench. She fumbles until her fingers close around it, lifts it above her head and strikes into the darkness with all her might. There's a thud and a scream, telling her that she hit Marico, but not hard enough to kill her.

Emma lifts the wrench again. She hits once more, but now the metal meets metal, and the wrench flies off to hit the ground somewhere in the dark.

Emma's left arm is as good as dead, and her hands are empty. She lost both the scalpel and the wrench, and she's got nothing left.

She struggles to control her breathing and tries to remember where the door should be, but she's lost her bearings. She reaches in the dark for the low shelf along the wall, then follows it. But, instead of the door, she finds herself at the bow. She turns around and heads back to where the door should be, holding her breath to hear better. But there's nothing but the hum of the engines. Three more steps and something moves to her left. She steps right, but it's too late. A ton of bricks crush her left foot, and she screams. The horrid pain makes her weak and dizzy, so she reaches to lean against the wall.

Shaking with pain and fear, she just wants to curl up and die. But she can't. She can't walk either, since her broken foot won't hold her, so she drops to the bench and struggles to control her breath until she hears a soft noise to her left.

She pushes herself forward and tackles Marico, who screams and falls with a thud. Emma rolls aside and waits, but nothing happens.

She holds her breath and reaches under the bench for the penlight but can't find it. She listens to the ominous silence, so creepy it gives her goosebumps. She must do something right now, or she'll die.

She crawls back to the door and finds the frame. She inhales and struggles to stand on her one good foot and pushes down the lever that opens the door just as a massive weight obliterates her right arm and crushes her to the ground.

The pain is like nothing Emma imagined, but even worse than that is the fear. She sees nothing but the menacing darkness and hears nothing but her own ragged breath. Somewhere in this terrible night, death is stalking her, and there's no stopping it. Death is here, whether Marico kills her or leaves her to die here alone.

Emma's fingers feel the rough floor and find something cold and smooth by her head. She pulls herself up, curls around it, and lays her cheek on it to cool her brain when a bright light fills the room.

Standing at the bow under the lantern, covered in blood from head to toe, Marico smiles. And that insane smile is even scarier than the cleaver she holds.

"You thought you'd get the better of me, didn't you. You thought you could outsmart me. Well, you were wrong. Nobody outsmarts me. Nobody."

Her smile bright white on her bloody face, she steps closer.

"See this cleaver? I sharpened it, especially for you. Remember I said I'd quarter you so I can throw you overboard? That was supposed to be after you were dead, but you just changed my mind.

"You hurt me. I made you a reasonable offer, and you tricked me and hurt me. Well, it's my turn.

"I'll hurt you like you've never been hurt before, and I'll love every moment. It will give me immense pleasure to cut you up alive. I'll start with your toes and move up. Slowly. Very slowly. I gave you a fair deal and offered you an easy death, but, as always, you had to be difficult. Well, doctor, let's see how you like this."

This can't be true, but it is. Locked inside this metal

dungeon with a homicidal maniac, with one broken leg and two arms out of commission, Emma ran out of time.

She's just three feet from the door, but she may as well be on the moon. Her feet won't let her run, and her arms won't protect her. Staring at a crazed Marico, Emma tries to squeeze behind the metal cylinder under the bench, but she knows she's at the end of the line.

Marico's pager goes off. She laughs.

"Time for your afternoon clinic, doctor. We'll miss you down there."

"You must have missed me at morning clinic too."

"Sure we did. I told them that I was worried about you. You haven't acted like yourself lately. You must be depressed or something. Sue laughed, but Fajar seemed concerned. I thought it was because he didn't want to work your clinic, but who knows? Maybe he really cares about you. Like he cares about his other women."

"I never had anything to do with Fajar, Marico."

"Of course not. And my mother is a bishop."

"That's the truth. I never had anything to do with Fajar."

"I saw him leaving your cabin after midnight."

"We just talked."

Marico laughs and lifts the cleaver above Emma's left foot.

"Ready?"

"Almost. One question?"

"What?"

"Why did you poison Amanda's parents? And how?"

"Oh, that. I almost forgot. I wanted to hurt that bitch like she had hurt me. And I hoped she'd be a suspect if they died. But they didn't. Thanks to you, of course. You had to stick your nose in that too."

"But they hadn't done anything to you! Why take innocent lives?"

"You call that a life? I was doing them a favor."

"And how did you do it?"

"Insecticides, of course. That's how we get rid of pests in the Philippines. OK, that's enough. Ready?"

With her left hand's trembling fingers, Emma pulls out the extinguisher's safety pin and pushes the button. The spray of white foam strikes Marico's face, filling her mouth and nose. Her crazy eyes go wide with shock as she slowly turns into a snowman. She drops the cleaver and the impact knocks her on her back.

Emma holds on to the extinguisher until it's empty.

She drops it aside and struggles to sit up. She crawls up to the bench, hops to the door and leans on it to push it open.

But it won't.

The door is locked.

She is locked in the dungeon, and whatever's left of Marico is locked in with her.

CHAPTER 57

My Dear Emma,

I'm so glad to hear that you are feeling better.

We've all been worried sick about you. It started the other night. Guinness was playing with Hope, but suddenly, she went berserk. She started growling and barking and wouldn't stop. I tried everything possible, but she wouldn't calm down, no matter what. I asked her what was going on. She looked into my eyes and told me to call you.

I know dogs don't talk, but I swear this one does. But you probably know it better than me.

I tried your cell phone, but you didn't answer. I called the ship. Don't even get me started on how hard it was to explain that I needed to speak to you immediately. They interrogated me to the seventh degree, and I had to tell them I was your mother and it was a matter of life and death. All this while Guinness barks like a maniac by the phone, and Hope screams like a banshee.

When they got tired of me, they connected me to Medical. I spoke to your friend Fajar, and I told him I was worried and asked him to find you.

He returned to tell me he couldn't find you, but he had initiated a thorough search all over the ship.

We were worried sick until you called back to tell me you had fallen on the steps. I'm glad you're doing OK, but please be more careful. You know stairs are dangerous, especially with the ship moving. Take it slow and be very careful.

Thank God you talked Guinness into calming down. I've never seen her so wound up. Who'd have guessed she could sense you're in trouble from thousands of miles away? But, to be honest, I'm not really that surprised. She seems to be talking to you often. I wonder if Hope will be part of the conclave.

I hope you enjoy your time in Thailand. I'm surprised they'll give you two weeks off for a couple of bruises, but I'm glad you have such a caring employer. I can't wait to see pictures and hear about Thai food and Thai markets.

I am happy to hear that your friend Frank will be going with you. I've heard good things about Thailand, but it's safer to not be alone. And who knows? It wouldn't hurt you to have a little fling.

We are well, though we all miss you, of course. Victor, Amber, and the girls send their love. Stay safe and stay in touch.

Love,

Margret

CHAPTER 58

The postcard-worthy green islands with snow-white beaches and palm trees swaying gently in the breeze make room for the concrete mass of Laem Chabang, the gate to Bangkok, Thailand's capital.

Hundreds of cranes line up against the morning sky like an army of zombies waiting to wake up. They are utilitarian and beautiful but scary. But it doesn't take much to scare Emma these days.

The good news is that the old nightmare with the blue-eyed man chasing her is gone. She only gets enough sleep for those where she fights Marico and the darkness. She gets them every night, so now she's afraid of the dark. She sleeps with the TV on, hoping the bluish light and monotonous sound will keep her grounded and chase away the monsters.

That night she fought Marico — or maybe day, who knows — taught her that she's got more fight in her than she thought.

It also taught her she can't fight forever.

That locked door hurt her more than any of Marico's

blows. She fell to the ground, curled up in a fetal position, and cried tears she couldn't afford since she was already dehydrated.

When the door finally opened and the security officers came in, she thought she was dreaming. But the pain searing through her body when they tried to pick her up told her they were real.

Dana and the stretcher team took her back to Medical, and Emma laughed when she saw Sue's face. I must look a wonder, she thought, glad she couldn't see herself.

"You'll live," Fajar said after examining her and checking her X-rays. "Two broken collarbones and a few fractured metatarsals won't kill you but will slow you down a bit. You need a few weeks off. We made arrangements to disembark you in Bangkok. You can fly back home if you want, but if I were you, I'd stay there. The flight back will take almost two days, and you'll be hurting. Why not stay in Thailand? Lovely weather, excellent food, and plenty of fun things to do."

"How is Marico?"

"You did a good job. Between the blood loss from the wounds and the freezing and choking her with the fire extinguisher, she's in worse shape than you are. I already shipped her to Bangkok; we'll see what they say. I'd say her chances are 50-50."

But now, sitting on the deck in her wheelchair, with her immobilized foot sticking forward, Emma wonders if disembarking in Bangkok was a good idea. What will she do with herself when she can't even walk?

Leaning on her cane by Emma's side, Hanna looks worried.

"You packed everything you need?"

"Except for what I forgot."

"No worries. In Bangkok you can find everything you want, from ice cream to stilettos," Fajar says, leaning against the railing with his hands in his pockets.

"Sure you can. If you can walk and use your hands," Hanna says.

"She can use her hands just fine; it's just the arms that give her trouble."

Emma laughs, but she's not sure how she'll manage in a foreign country where she doesn't even speak the language with both arms in slings and a cast on her foot.

Frank shrugs. "No worries. I'll take care of everything. I'll hire a car to take her places, I'll make sure she doesn't go hungry, and I'll keep her company, so she doesn't get bored."

Hanna's blue eyes sparkle with glee.

"What a Don Juan. She had to break both her arms and a foot before you could nab her."

"It's not my fault she wanted nothing to do with me when she could walk. One's got to do what one's got to do."

The gangplank opens, and a smiling steward wheels Emma down the gangplank to the pier. Since she's disabled, she gets to go first, with the VIPs. She glances back to the *Sea Horse* crawling with passengers about to disembark. Fajar and Hanna wave at her from the deck.

"Have fun! See you soon."

Emma nods and smiles, and the steward wheels her through immigration.

She's waiting for Frank when a light hand touches her back. It's Nok, resplendent in her red sundress and hat.

"Isn't that fortunate? I'll get to show you Bangkok after all."

"I'm not sure that fortunate is the right word."

"Good enough for me."

Nok smiles at Frank's frown.

"You thought you'd have her all to yourself? Not exactly, my friend. I'm here too, and I plan to show her a thing or two."

CHAPTER 59

Dear Mother,

I'm glad to hear that you feel better and enjoy Thailand. I looked it up on YouTube, and it looks fascinating. How do you like the food? Is it as hot as they say? Have you visited the floating markets? How about Soi Cowboy? One of my school buddies is half Thai, and he says that the lady-boys are prettier than most women and that you'd never know they are boys unless you checked their you-know-whats. Is that true?

We are well. Hope grows every day, and she won't stop talking. She doesn't say any words, but she babbles all the time, though nobody understands what she says. Nobody but Guinness, that is. The two of them are thick as thieves, and Grandma and I feel a bit left out.

School is OK, though kinda boring. But I do my best to stick with it. I decided to go premed and then go to medical school like Dad.

He told me to give you my regards and say he misses you and wishes you a speedy recovery and a great time in Bangkok.

I have to run to my Chemistry lab.

Taylor

P.S. When are you coming home? We miss you.

PPS. What's the best thing about your trip?

Emma pushes her laptop aside. It's been just a couple of months since she left home, but it feels like forever. And she can't remember Taylor ever missing her, in her eighteen years. Maybe the little devil is finally growing up?

She shuffles to the bathroom leaning on her cane. She struggles a little, but manages to gather her hair in a clasp, then puts on the new wine-colored lipstick Nok got her and examines herself in the mirror.

The nights without her pager and the days of fun in the sun have done wonders. Her skin glows, and she feels younger than she's been in years.

She checks her watch. Fifteen minutes to get downstairs for the tour Frank organized. She doesn't know what it is, but it will be fun. Frank's plans always are. And his eternal squabbles with Nok make them even more so.

She smiles and sits at the desk.

"My dear Taylor,

I'm happy to hear that you girls are well. I miss you too and can't wait to see you all again.

Congratulations on deciding on Medicine, like your father. He loves it. I hope it will be the same for you.

I haven't visited the floating market, since getting in and out of boats with a cane is a challenge. But I've been to Soi Cowboy, and the performers are spectacular, even though I haven't checked their you-know-whats to know precisely what they are. But, by their deep voices and Adam's apples, I wouldn't be too surprised if they had something tucked in.

Give my best regards to your father and Amber, and kiss Hope and Grandma for me. And give Guinness a nice marrow bone.

Love,
Mother
P.S. I don't know.
PPS. I love it all — my fun new friends, the fantastic food, the exciting places. But the best thing about my trip was discovering that I don't really need anyone to feel whole. I'm happy on my own.

Emma clicks send, then realizes she lied. She needs someone to feel complete.

She needs Guinness.

~

TO FIND out more about Emma, Frank and Nok, and to follow Emma on her next life-changing adventure, read *SEE EVIL.*

~

WHAT IF THE person who's supposed to save your life is actually trying to end it? Find out in *ER CRIMES*, the chilling medical thriller series that will leave you breathless.

AFTERWORD

Thank you for reading *DO HARM*. If you enjoyed it, please leave a review to help other readers like you.

Guinness fans: check out **BECOMING K-9** A Bomb Dog's Tale. It's her heartwarming memoir that will pull at your heartstrings. It's also the book I'm most proud of.

ABOUT THE AUTHOR

Rada was born in Transylvania, ten miles from Dracula's Castle. Growing up between communists and vampires taught her that humans are fickle, but you can always rely on dogs and books. That's why she read every book she could get, including the phone book (too many characters, not enough plot), and adopted every stray she found, from dogs to frogs.

After joining her American husband, she spent years studying medicine and working in the ER and on cruise ships all over the world, but she still speaks like Dracula's cousin.

And, while the characters and situations in Do Harm are fictional, the ports of call, the medical cases, and the snippets from the crews' lives are based on Rada's personal experience.

facebook.com/RadaJonesMD

bookbub.com/profile/rada-jones

instagram.com/RadaJonesMD

x.com/JonesRada

OTHER BOOKS BY RADA JONES

 **ER CRIMES Series :** What if the one supposed to save your life is trying to end it? Find out in *'ER Crimes,'* the chilling thriller series that will leave you breathless.

K-9 HEROES Series: "Until you, hoomans, learn to sniff each other's butts so you can read each other's thoughts, you'll need us, dogs, to guide you, love you, and make you better people."

≈

 **STAY AWAY FROM MY ER:** Not for the faint of heart... You'll laugh, cry, and marvel at the ER'a alien world.

≈

DRIVING ITALY: Two intrepid curmudgeons. An SUV with red plates. Ten thousand miles of twisty roads. What could go wrong?

EXCERPT FROM BECOMING K-9

Who knew training humans was so hard? You'd wonder why. They aren't that stupid. It takes them a while, but they eventually learn when you want out, you're hungry or you're thirsty. They can even talk to each other by making noise with their tongue. How weird is that? Even my brother Blue, who's the slowest of us all, knows that the tongue is for lapping water and panting to cool down.

Mom cocked her head and licked my nose.

"That's the best they can do, dear. They have no tails, their ears don't move, and most don't even have enough fur to raise their hackles. No wonder they're confused and need us to guide them. And that's what we do; that's our life's work. But we need to choose them carefully."

Mom was on her sixth litter and very wise. Beautiful, too, with her long muzzle, amber eyes, and smooth, shiny fur, all black but for her golden legs and loving pink tongue.

She glanced at Yellow, who chased his tail instead of paying attention, and growled. He hung his head and sat in line with the rest of us to listen.

It was a lovely summer day as Mom homeschooled us in

Jones's front yard. The warm wind tickled my nose. I bit it, but I caught nothing. I tried again, but Mother threw me a side glance, so I closed my mouth and sat still.

"Boys and girls, today's the day. People will come to check you out and choose which one to take home. They don't know it, but it doesn't work that way. You choose your humans, but choose them wisely. Sniff them all, then pick the ones that smell like food if you want a good life. You may sometimes get bacon, maybe even grapes. Humans say dogs don't eat grapes, but that's poppycock. They just want to keep them for themselves. My grandma was a pure-bred Alsatian, and she loved Riesling. I never had Riesling, but Concord isn't bad."

A shiny strip of drool dripped from Mom's mouth. She licked it off and inspected us. We were seven: three boys and four girls. But that doesn't much matter when you're just ten weeks old. The only difference is how you pee. The boys don't know how to squat so they need something to lift their leg to, like a bush or a mailbox. How stupid!

"Why don't you just lift your leg, if that's what you need to do? What does the bush have to do with anything?"

Mom bristled.

"Leave them alone, Red."

I tried, but it was hard. I was the runt of the litter, so I had to prove myself all the time. Mom said I had a Napoleonic complex.

"What's that?"

"It's when you're the smallest, so you have to be meaner to show them that size doesn't matter."

I told you Mom is brilliant. She came all the way from Germany when she was just a pup. Our human, Jones, has two passions: German shepherds and history. Mom was his first German shepherd, and he spent lots of time teaching her things most dogs never heard about.

He still does, even now that she's old. He sits in his recliner and reads to her as she lays by the fireplace. Sometimes I listen in. There was a story about a dude named Hitler. Not a nice guy, but for loving German shepherds. Another one about that short guy Napoleon who tried to conquer the world while wearing funny hats. And one about some place called Afghanistan.

"That's a bad war, Maddie," Jones said, scratching the four white hairs in his beard. "Those Taliban, they are not nice people."

He calls her Maddie, but her real name is Madeline Rose Kahn Van Jones. He is Jones. The Van is for Van Gogh, some orange dude who got so mad he bit off his own ear. The rest is just for show, since people pay more for dogs with long names; they call that a pedigree. Mom's pedigree is longer than her tail.

As always, Mom was right. People came to see us, and they brought their spouses, their kids, and even their dogs to check us out and choose which one to get. Like, really? Jones said that only one out of twenty German shepherd owners is smarter than his dog. I don't believe it. I bet he fudged the numbers to feel better. You think you own a dog? Who feeds who? Who cleans after who? Who does the work, everything but making decisions? You, human, in case you didn't know it. You don't buy a dog; you hire supervision. But I digress.

My littermates and I wore colored collars so humans could tell us apart. There was no need, really, since we were all different, but humans couldn't see it. What color did I wear? Red, of course. I was small, but I was the queen of the litter, whether the others liked it or not.

A fat man in a Hawaiian shirt stopped to stare at me. He called his female.

"Look at this red one! Isn't he cute?"

She hobbled closer, leaning on her crooked stick. I love sticks, so I tried to take it. She didn't want to let go, but I insisted. They laughed.

"Let's get him."

Jones cleared his throat.

"Red is lovely, indeed, but she's a very active little person who needs a lot of attention. How much time do you plan to work with her every day?"

"Work with her?"

"Yes. Walk her, train her, and play with her."

They stared at him like he'd lost his marbles. He smiled.

"May I recommend Brown here? He's lovely, easygoing, and eager to please. He'll be happy to lay on the sofa watching TV. Or Miss Green? She's a polite little lady who gets along with everyone and never disappoints."

Brown left. So did Green, Yellow, and even White, while I stayed, waiting for my forever home.

"Take it easy, Red dear," Mother said when there were only two of us left—Black and me. "You need to soften up a bit; otherwise, you'll be left without a family. People look for easygoing dogs to fit into their lives, not for somebody to take charge. Though maybe they should, really, but they aren't smart enough to know that."

Her German accent made her words feel harsh. Have you ever listened to Germans? It's like they're constipated while they also have a cold. They keep clearing their throats, so their words come out like bullets from a machine gun. I don't speak German, but I love watching old war movies with Jones.

"What do you mean, Mom? What should I do?"

"Lick their hands, sweetheart. Wrap yourself around their feet and stare at them like they hung the moon."

"Are you serious?"

"Of course."

"But they're stupid!"

"Come on, Red, don't be so judgmental. You're just a pup, and you have so much to learn. A nice family will give you a good life. They'll love you, play with you, and spoil you. Knowing you have a good, safe home will lift a weight off my soul."

You think I listened? You've got to be kidding.

That's how I ended up in the military.

Read BECOMING K-9

Made in the USA
Columbia, SC
02 January 2025

51072371R00181